The Hanging Party

One of the posse slipped the free end of the rope through its hondo, and dropped the loop over the head of the blond boy.

Longarm looked around, but the two local law officers had walked off into the darkness somewhere, literally turning their backs on the situation at the campfire.

Even if he no longer considered himself a peace officer, Longarm damn sure considered himself a man.

He stepped forward.

"Whoa," he said in a low voice. "You boys don't know what you're doing . . ."

"You son of a bitch." The man was drunk with the scent of blood. "We'll just hang them—an' you too . . ."

Longarm slowed him down with a close look at the business end of a .44 Colt.

—◆— TABOR EVANS —◆—

LONGARM

AND THE BIG POSSE

J

JOVE BOOKS, NEW YORK

LONGARM AND THE BIG POSSE

A Jove Book / published by arrangement with
the author

PRINTING HISTORY
Jove edition / September 1987

ISBN: 0-515-09169-3

PRINTED IN THE UNITED STATES OF AMERICA

10 9 8 7 6 5 4 3 2 1

Chapter 1

Longarm paused and reached into his coat pocket for a cheroot. It was not that he especially wanted a smoke again so soon. He had only tossed the last one away in the last block. But he did want a moment to admire the most attractive young lady who was climbing into a hack at the curbside on Denver's Colfax Avenue.

He nipped off the end of the cheroot and spat out the fleck of tobacco, then bent over a cupped match, pretending to concentrate on his smoke while his eyes locked unerringly on the shapely flash of ankle that was displayed while the woman was handed into the cab by a driver who seemed every bit as appreciative of his cargo as Longarm was.

The lady was a tall brunette, most nicely put together. For a moment Longarm fantasized a past for her, a nearly complete identity, even something of a future.

She was in this businesslike part of town, he decided, to see an attorney about a divorce. Unusual, perhaps, but certainly not unheard of. She was wealthy. That was it. And her philandering husband had been squandering her funds. She was bereft by the necessity for the public spectacle of divorce. Surely now she would require comforting in her time of great need.

Longarm thought he might know someone who would be willing to provide that comfort.

He sighed audibly as the hack driver latched the cab door closed. The fool. She was just settling onto the seat and had not yet arranged her skirts.

The driver climbed back onto the open seat of his hackney, took up his lines, and shook the horse into motion.

Longarm stood where he was, drawing on the unwanted cheroot, while the cab rolled away and turned the corner past the Denver Mint.

Such lovely possibilities gone to waste.

Still, the little episode made Longarm feel a bit better. This morning he *needed* something to make him feel better.

Almost anything would have helped.

He was tired.

More than that, he was just plain soul-weary.

That was it, really. It was something closer to depression of the spirit than fatigue of bone and muscle.

This last assignment had not been a pleasant one.

Oh, he had accomplished it, all right. But there was little pleasure in knowing that Johnny McFee was in federal custody. The miserable little son of a bitch had gone on a rampage at the last moment. Stole funds from the U.S. Post Office, discovered that the money would not buy him the happiness he sought, and then vented his frustrations on innocent passersby on the street before Longarm reached the town to put him in irons. Two men died in that bloody affair, and there was a blameless youngster still in a coma who might or might not recover from the bullet McFee's careless ricochet had put into him.

Damn the fellow, anyway. And the worst part of it was that once Longarm showed up and announced himself as a

2

federal officer, the sorry little bastard had thrown down his guns, thrown up his hands, and turned himself over without a hint of resistance.

It was perfectly all right for him to mow down innocents. But not for Johnny himself to become at risk. Never that.

The whole affair had left a sour taste in Longarm's throat. Almost as sour as the unwanted cheroot he was now putting in his mouth.

Angrily, feeling low again, Deputy U.S. Marshal Custis Long flung his barely lighted cheroot into the gutter and proceeded up the steps of the Federal Building and into Marshal Billy Vail's office.

Longarm was in no mood for flippancy this morning. Instead of tossing a wisecrack toward the clerk, Henry, who sat at the outer desk in the marshal's office and then flipping his Stetson toward the rack in the corner, Longarm muttered a greeting to Henry—no point in taking things out on him—and crossed the room to hang his hat where it properly belonged. That simple gesture was enough to make Henry's eyebrows rise in unspoken inquiry, but Longarm did not feel up to explanations.

"Is the boss in?" he asked.

"Of course." That was one thing about Marshal Vail. He was no paper-pushing political appointee. He was a damned fine administrator who had been an even finer field man in his day, and it was considered a late arrival for him if he failed to show up for work half an hour before the posted hours of his office. "Did you want to see him?" Henry asked.

Longarm nodded. "If he isn't too busy. Got a report to turn in." He reached inside his coat and produced a slim sheaf of papers already written out and carefully folded, ready for submission. Paperwork was not one of Custis Long's long suits. Having him submit a report without being hounded for it was almost unheard of in this office. Henry blinked but said nothing beyond "I'll tell him you're here."

Wordlessly Longarm nodded and took a seat on one of

the hardbacked wooden chairs arranged along the wall.

Henry pushed aside the files he had been going over, rose, and slipped silently through the door into Billy Vail's private office.

He was in there for several long moments before he reappeared and motioned Longarm inside.

"Yes?" Vail asked cheerfully once Longarm had the door closed behind him and was standing in front of his old friend's desk without helping himself to a seat.

"The report on the McFee thing," Longarm said. He dropped the papers in front of Vail. "It's all . . . it's all in there. McFee is in custody. I brought him in last night."

Vail nodded. "I saw him listed on the arrivals sheet this morning. Good work."

Good work, indeed. It was a dead simple deal. Just take the train over there, snap the cuffs in place, and escort the prisoner back to Denver. Big deal. If it *hadn't* gone so smoothly he would have been in line for an ass-chewing, maybe. But "good work"? The entire thing hadn't taken twenty-four hours.

Was it so very obvious, the way he was feeling now?

Must be, or Billy and that damned tale-carrying Henry wouldn't be acting this way.

Longarm would have objected, but he simply did not feel up to an argument at the moment.

"Look . . . Billy . . . ," he said haltingly, "I think . . . I mean, I know that you're busy right now. You probably want me to dash out on something else. Stay good and busy. Go chase people or shoot somebody. I know that. But . . ."

Vail held a palm up to cut short the disjointed flow of talk.

"As a matter of fact," Billy Vail said, "we're having a lull right now. Smiley finally got a line on Bertram Walker, so he and some of the boys are down in Trinidad to finish that off. That is the only big case we have pending just now. The only thing remaining would be some routine warrant services, prisoner transport, that sort of thing. Actually, I was thinking just yesterday that this might be a good time for you to get some of your leave time off the books. You've been piling it up too deep lately. If you don't take a little personal time off soon, lad, the auditors will be after me. Too much accumulation and they get nervous, you know. It would be a good idea if you were to take a few weeks of vacation. Go fishing, whatever. Would you be willing to do that?"

Lordy, it *must* be obvious, then. Longarm had never in his life seen a manure spreader that was as full of shit as that speech had been.

Slow time, indeed. There was a train robbery in Wyoming. An assault on government officials in New Mexico Territory. That tip they got about some Indian agent defrauding his wards . . . Hell, those were just the ones Longarm could think of off the top of his head. Likely there were a dozen more that he didn't know about. And there were always liquor violations on the reservations, that sort of thing. Billy could double his field staff and still not keep up with it all.

And calling him *lad?*

That wasn't like Vail.

Longarm sighed. Maybe he *did* need some time to himself. It had been . . . right offhand, he couldn't remember the last time he had taken a real vacation.

Lord knew he could use one now.

And maybe there was something to this business about the pencil-pushers not liking a man to build up too much vacation time. Billy certainly said it like it was so.

Right now, Longarm had no idea how much time he had coming to him. No idea at all.

"I'll tell you what, Longarm. You could do me a big favor two ways here. Keep those auditors off my back by taking some free time, and help me get a prisoner moved too." There was a forced, false-ringing heartiness in Billy's voice now. As if he realized Longarm was onto his deception and he was trying to cover it, or at least to make his suggestions palatable by pretending they were more in the line of duty.

"What d'you want me to do, Billy?" Longarm was not

in a mood to argue his boss's transparent ploy.

Whatever it was, he would do it.

Right now, he truly did not care.

"Well, you see, I'd consider it a favor if you could take Dewey Bright over to Omaha for me. The man's trial starts in a few weeks, and I've been wondering who to break loose and send him with. You could do that. Tomorrow. Whenever. It would give you a reason to travel on your government pass. And then you could take some time for yourself instead of coming straight back."

Transparent? No more so than a pane of window glass. Billy knew damn good and well that his best deputy had an old flame in Omaha. A certain lady with high social standing but a passionate disregard for conventional mores.

Longarm's lips thinned. Not into a smile, exactly. But not all that far from it, either.

"I could do that," he said.

Vail smiled. "Good man. I'll send the paperwork over to the jail this morning. You can pick Bright up and transport him at your convenience."

Longarm sighed again. Such a big favor he was doing for Billy. Sure he was. He remembered Dewey Bright, although the man's arrest had not been Longarm's case. Bright was a penny-ante embezzler. The sort of meek, mild, inoffensive fellow who probably would go quietly to trial by himself if somebody handed him a railroad ticket and told him to show up at the Omaha courthouse on the appointed day.

Oh, well. Whatever the excuses and whatever the pretenses, Billy and Henry were genuinely concerned about him. They were honestly trying to help him out when he was low. That was something to remember and to be grateful for.

Longarm stood. "Thanks, Billy."

"Hey, thank *you*. It's you who's doing me the favor, remember?"

Longarm very nearly smiled at that. He stood there for a moment, then turned and moved toward the door.

"Custis?"

He stopped and turned back to look at Vail, whose bald pate was gleaming from the sunlight coming through the window behind his desk. "Yeah, Billy?"

"Take as much time as you need coming back. No hurry about it."

"Thanks, Billy."

In the outer office he paused in front of Henry's desk, stood there for a moment in silence.

But there was really nothing he could say to the slender, bespectacled clerk. A thank-you would have been an admission that the lean, ferociously mustachioed deputy did not want to make.

"Take care of yourself, Henry."

"What?"

Longarm retrieved his Stetson and headed for the front door.

"Uh, you too, Longarm."

But by then Longarm was already out in the hallway and heading for the street.

Funny thing, but he did not really feel any better for having some free time on his hands.

Maybe with luck there would be another cab and another attractive young lady to take his mind off things. To help him forget the stupidity and the futility that were weighing him down. The stupidity of criminality. And the futility that had to be felt by any son of a bitch dumb enough to think he could make a difference.

Chapter 2

"Custis! Custis! Wake up now."

Longarm snorted and coughed, coming reluctantly back from sleep. His mouth tasted foul from the smoke of too many cheroots, and there was a stab of pain from a cramp in his neck from sleeping sitting upright on the thinly padded Union Pacific seat.

He opened his eyes, blinked, and made out the concerned face of Dewey Bright leaning close over him. His prisoner had him by the arm and was shaking him lightly.

"What is it, Dewey?"

"We're coming into Omaha. The conductor just came through to announce the station. You said you wanted to know."

Bright acted as if he was worried he might have done something wrong. "You did say that, Custis."

"So I did." Longarm stiffled a yawn and rubbed his

knuckles across tired eyes. He had slept, but he had not rested. "Thanks, Dewey."

He and his prisoner had been on a first-name basis almost from the moment Longarm signed for custody of Bright at the Denver County jail. Longarm yawned again and sat upright. His eyes felt like soot or grit of some kind had collected under the lids while he was sleeping. And he wished his bag was up here in the passenger car instead of back in the baggage car. He was wanting his bottle of rye whiskey to take some of the foulness off his tongue.

"Are you all right, Custis? Can I get you anything?"

Damn. A prisoner asking in all sincerity if *he* could get *Longarm* anything?

The odd thing about it was that he believed Dewey was sincere. The man was a criminal—well, an alleged criminal; the proof still had to be presented in a court of law—but he was hardly the type to be a threat to anyone. He seemed just a happy, well-meaning, amiable sort who had "borrowed" just a bit more from his office accounts than he could repay. It was only the fact that he had been working as a Homestead Act agency clerk that made the escapade a federal matter and therefore a major offense. Hell, if he had been working in some county office in an organized state instead of a federally administered territory, the locals probably would have chided him and made him promise to pay back the missing money. And he would have done it.

Longarm couldn't bring himself to hate the man.

"No. Nothing, thanks."

"If you're sure." Dewey was continuing to look at him with concern.

"Positive," Longarm said. He shifted forward in his seat, tugged at the tweed coat that had bunched behind him while he slept and that now was probably hopelessly wrinkled, and reached for a cheroot. "Care for one?"

Dewey Bright shook his head.

"You don't smoke at all?"

Dewey shook his head again. "Nor drink," he said primly.

Longarm smiled. "But you do have other vices."

10

Bright snickered, then blushed a deep, bright red. "That's why I did it, you know."

"I didn't know."

"Oh, yes. Very foolish, I'm sure. Which you tall, good-looking fellows wouldn't understand. Not looking like me, I mean."

Bright did have something of a point there, probably. He was short and a good thirty pounds beyond being merely chunky. He was fat, actually, and going bald.

Longarm, on the other hand, had a horseman's build, broad of shoulder but with narrow hips, and was ruggedly handsome with his dark-tanned features, brown hair, and thick brown moustache.

"That has something to do with why you took the money, Dewey?"

"Oh, yes. It was for Theresa." Bright got a distant look about him as he thought back to his Theresa. "She liked me, you see. But she had very expensive tastes. And I had a very small salary." He smiled. "Everyone says I did a wrong thing, and I am sure they are correct. But it was worth it." •

"At least you aren't trying to lie your way out of it, Dewey. I like that about you."

"I am *not* a liar, Custis. I may be a lot of things, but I'm no liar."

"You're all right, Dewey."

"Thank you, Custis." The man seemed genuinely pleased.

Any other prisoner Longarm had ever been around would have taken that as an opportunity to ask the deputy for a good word, as a left-handed character witness or something, on his behalf. But Dewey Bright made no such suggestion. Longarm decided he would have to drop a word into someone's ear for Dewey anyway.

Probably the poor fellow didn't know enough to make the request.

Longarm hid another yawn behind his fist as the U.P. eastbound began to clank and jolt in compression. The engine slowed and the brakemen had to work to set the

11

wheels on the rest of the cars.

A glance through the soot-grimed window beside Dewey showed that they were already passing through the outskirts of Omaha. Soon they would reach the stockyards and then, quickly, the depot. The train was moving no faster now than a man could run.

"Reckon we can start getting ourselves together," Longarm said.

He pulled his watch out of his vest pocket, dipped two fingers deep inside the pocket, and came up with the handcuff key that he had hidden there after letting Bright "see" him put the key in a trousers pocket instead.

He unlocked the cuff he had snapped around the arm of the coach seat and returned the key to his trousers pocket. Dewey rubbed industriously at his wrist, although Longarm had been careful not to snap the steel manacle on too tightly.

"I'm sorry if that bothers you," Longarm said, "but I have to follow procedure."

"Oh, I understand that. Goodness, I shouldn't want you to get into any trouble."

"I'll give you a minute to get your circulation back. Then I'll have to put it back on your other wrist."

"All right." The loose cuff dangled free while Dewey rubbed at his wrist with his other hand. Longarm felt sorry for the chubby fellow. Still . . .

The train had been dragging against the brakes with loud squeals of protest. Now it jolted to a halt. The other passengers in the coach quickly stood and reached for bags and lunch baskets as they prepared to leave the train. Longarm was in no hurry to get off the train. He was willing to wait while the aisle cleared.

"Oh, dear," Dewey said. "Surely that can't be Theresa up there . . ."

"Where?"

Longarm looked toward the front of the coach. The only female he could see was a plump, dowdy woman in her fifties who had ridden with them in the coach all the way from Julesburg. "I don't see—"

12

A flash of gleaming metal flickered briefly in the corner of Longarm's eye.

He jerked back, and the slashing handcuffs swept past his nose to slam painfully down across his chest.

Had the hard-whipped steel connected, it would have laid his scalp open or worse.

Longarm clamped a hand down toward the butt of his Colt, riding in its crossdraw holster at his waist, and found Dewey's other hand already there, fumbling for a grip on the .44 caliber revolver.

Longarm took a firm hold on Dewey's wrist and squeezed, at the same time driving an elbow sideways into Dewey's ribs.

The fat man gasped, and all the strength seemed to go out of him.

He sagged back in his seat, pasty white now from the shock of impact from where Longarm hit him.

"Here now, Custis. You didn't have to be so rough." He actually sounded offended.

Dewey withdrew his hand from the butt of Longarm's Colt and Longarm motioned for him to slide forward and turn.

"Really, Custis. There's no need to cuff them behind my back. After all, I—"

"Shut up, Dewey."

Since picking Bright up at the jail, Longarm had allowed the man the relative freedom and comfort of having his wrists cuffed in front of him or of being attached to the railroad seat by only the one hand. The repayment had not exactly been in the coin of gratitude. From now on the sneaky bastard could manage with his wrists cuffed behind his back, and to hell with him.

"Really, Custis. I had to try it. Surely you can understand that, and forgive . . ."

But Longarm wasn't listening to him any more. Instead he was mentally berating himself for allowing Bright to make such a damn fool of him.

Here Billy Vail had gone and given his top deputy the easiest, simplest, most foulup-proof job in the book. And

13

Custis Long had turned right around and tried to fuck it up.

If that wasn't a warning to him . . .

Longarm shook his head sadly.

If this kept up, maybe he should take a permanent vacation from duty.

Not just take his time about going back, but mail in a resignation.

If a meek little fellow like Dewey Bright could try him and damn near get away with it, maybe Custis Long's malaise had gone too deep to be corrected.

Maybe this depression of his was just too deeply rooted this time to overcome.

Maybe the smart thing would be to find Lucille Whitacker here in Omaha and see if she wanted a *permanent* houseguest. She had hinted as much the last time they were together.

Well, maybe he should take her up on it. Just send Billy a letter of resignation, crawl into Lucille's bed, and pull a bottle in with him. And let the world go to hell without him having to fret about it.

Maybe, by damn, that just wouldn't be a half-bad idea.

"Watch the step there. Don't fall," Longarm said automatically as Dewey Bright, handcuffs clamped behind him, made his way out of the U.P. coach and down the iron steps to the platform. "No, not that way. We got to go back to the baggage car for our things. That's it. Watch your step now."

Bright was saying something, trying to explain himself, but Longarm was not listening.

All he wanted now was to turn the prisoner over to the proper authorities in Omaha and then take a fast cab to Lucille's. He wouldn't even stop along the way to buy a supply of liquor. Surely her cabinet would be well stocked. If not, she could damn well send out for something. He intended to hit that front door this afternoon and not budge outside it again for two weeks.

Or longer.

Or maybe never.

But why oh *why* wasn't anything going right any more.

14

Chapter 3

Longarm stepped out of the jail, signed receipt for Dewey Bright in his pocket, and hailed a cab. His customary traveling kit of carpetbag, saddle, and scabbarded Winchester were back at the railroad depot checked with the station clerk. He had not felt like juggling them and trying to handle Dewey too after the man's abortive attempt to get away nor did he want to take the time to fool with them now. He could send for the gear later. *After* he saw Lucille and got the better part of a bottle of Maryland rye under his belt.

Lordy, but he had never felt like this before. Didn't want to now; didn't want to again in the future.

This was just . . . He shook his head absently as the cab driver came to a halt before him.

The driver misunderstood the unconscious gesture and started to drive away. Longarm called him back with a curt bark of anger.

"But I thought . . ."

"Never mind. Just take me to . . . shit, what's the address. . . . just take me up on Bluff Road. I'll point the way from there."

"Yes, sir," the cabby said dubiously.

Longarm climbed inside the rig, uncaring what this stranger might think, and settled back on the hard seat.

It would all be better once he got to Lucille's. That, at least, was something he could be sure of.

He had known Lucille . . . what . . . three years? Just short of that now. Met her in Denver at one of those damnable duty affairs. She was as bored as he was that night, and the two of them escaped together. Spent a long weekend in her hotel room that time and had managed to get together again for a weekend or simply a day every now and then since. Mostly in Denver, but once in a while here in Omaha.

Lucille was not much of a talker. Now that he thought about it, he realized that he really knew rather little about her.

Oh, he knew the important things. The feel of her, cool and crisp when she first came to him, warm and limp as he left her. Knew the scents and the textures of her. The scent of her bathing soap and her powders. The muskier odors of her flesh after an evening of lovemaking. The softness of the hollow of her throat and the incredible, almost fierce strength of her arms and her legs in passion.

As for her background, he knew very little, despite the amount of time they had spent together.

They had really spoken very little, either of them. She knew in a vague sort of way that he did something for the government. He knew that she was a lady of wealth.

Beyond that . . . He shrugged. Beyond that, he truly did not care at this particular moment.

The cab left the business district of Omaha and rolled at a brisk trot through one residential neighborhood after another, each block offering facades taller and more elegant than the last until they finally reached a section Longarm remembered from his last visit here. He leaned forward to slide open the panel that separated him from the driver's box. "Turn right here."

"Which way, sir?"

"Right, damn it. Didn't I just tell you that!"

"No, sir, you . . . never mind, sir." The cab wheeled to the right, passing between a pair of tall stone columns that guarded a block of exclusive mansions.

"On the left," Longarm said. "That second house there."

"Yes, sir." Iron tires crunched over gravel as the cab swung into the drive, and the driver used a combination of rein and whip to collect his nag into a respectably high-stepping gait as he brought the rig to a halt before the porch of the magnificent house.

Longarm grunted with something close to satisfaction and waited while the cabby jumped down to open the door for him and hand him down onto firm ground again. He paid the man, tipping him a bit for the extra courtesy, and brushed at the sleeves of his brown tweed coat before he made for the door of the mansion.

"Should I wait, sir?"

"No," Longarm told him. "No need for that."

"Very good, sir." The cabby sounded impressed. Quickly he climbed back onto his driving box and made a swift, flourishing exit back onto the street.

Longarm watched him go, then mounted the broad steps to the porch and raised the massive, cast brass knocker. Within moments he heard footsteps inside.

"Suh?" The butler who answered the knock was tall and cadaverously thin. Longarm remembered the fellow from previous visits to this house, yet there was no smile of welcome, not so much as an acknowledgement of recognition on the carefully neutral expression the man displayed. Longarm was not sure if he should be annoyed by that or if he should be impressed by the butler's attention to the details of duty.

"Custis Long to call on Miss Whitacker," Longarm said formally.

Still there was no recognition on the butler's face. Longarm remembered now that his name was Albert. He continued to look like he had just been sucking a lemon.

"Mrs. Vandellenberg is not available to callers at the moment, suh," Albert said, his eyes focused somewhere a good dozen feet behind Longarm's head. "Shall I announce you to the master instead?"

"To . . . ?"

"To the master, suh. That would be Mr. Carlton Vandellenberg the Third, suh. Do you wish to pay your respects to Mr. Vandellenberg, Mr. Long?"

"Oops." Longarm fumbled inside his coat for a cheroot and tried to light it without first biting off the tip, corrected that error, and tried again with better results. "Uh, tell me, Albert, Mrs. Vandellenberg would be . . . ?"

"Mrs. Vandellenberg, suh, would be the former Miz Whitacker." There was a flicker of something in Albert's eyes that might have been sympathy, or might as easily have been masked contempt. Longarm really was not sure.

"No," he said. "I . . . uh, I don't believe I want to call on the master. Right now."

"As you wish, suh." With a nod and half a bow, Albert withdrew a step backward and swung the huge door gently but firmly shut in Longarm's face.

Be damned, Longarm told himself as he turned and looked blankly back toward the city. Had it been *that* long since he had heard from Lucille? Apparently it had.

Now he was wishing he hadn't been so quick to dismiss the cab.

On the other hand, better to have a hike while he tried to sort through this than face the humiliation of having *two* strangers see him in the predicament.

Longarm clamped the end of his cheroot in his teeth and began the long walk back toward the U.P. depot.

He sure as hell was having fun on his vacation, he reflected as he walked.

The U.P. passenger rumbled westward, a rhythmic jolting and clacking rocking the sooty car as the wheel trucks met rail joints. Longarm reached into the carpetbag on the seat

18

beside him and brought out the bottle of rye, pulled the cork, and took a deep swallow of the fiery liquor. The whiskey flowed into his belly, spreading warmth there but no relief from a depression that was of the mind and not the body. The carpetbag and the bottle had been kept close to hand ever since the train pulled out of Omaha.

"Bitch," he mumbled without meaning it.

Longarm's problem was not Lucille Whitacker. No, not Whitacker any longer. Something else now. He did not try to remember what the name was these days. No point in remembering that.

He knew good and well that Lucille was not at fault. He had felt this way long before he learned about her.

Besides, she was entitled to her happiness, whatever it might be and wherever it might lead her.

That really wasn't it at all.

His problem was . . . What the hell *was* his problem anyway? He honestly didn't know. And the truth was that right now he did not particularly *want* to know. He simply felt like shit, clear down to the marrow of his bones.

He took another drink from the ever-handy bottle in the ever-handy bag and tried to forget about Lucille Whitacker and Billy Vail and Dewey Bright and assholes like Johnny McFee and everything.

The bag was handy; the bottle was handy; they could just stay that way.

Once, only once, some overdressed fool of a traveling drummer had thought to take the seat beside Longarm, had actually reached down to lay hands on Longarm's carpetbag and move the bag to an overhead rack.

The man had seen the icy glare Long gave him and moved quietly to the next coach back. There had not been a word exchanged between them. None had been necessary. Since then not even the conductor had approached Longarm. The conductor saw Longarm's pass when the tall deputy boarded the train. He had not approached Long since.

"Fuck 'em," Longarm mumbled to himself. He heard the slur in his voice but did not care.

He could sit there and get drunk if he damn well wanted to.

Nothing wrong with that, was there?

Hell, no.

Man should have another drink on that thought, shouldn't he?

Longarm thought maybe he should.

He had another drink on it, although he was not entirely clear on just why he was doing it. Celebrating something? Good idea to celebrate if a son of a bitch had something to celebrate.

As for himself, well, he didn't have much cause to celebrate anything lately, did he?

No? Shit, have another drink anyway. Celebrate *not* having anything to celebrate.

He had another drink.

Damn bottle was about empty. Cheatin' sons of bitches couldn't even put a decent amount o' liquor in a bottle.

He tilted the offensive bottle to the side of his mouth and spilled a little of the smooth rye down his chin as he killed the last of it.

He tossed the empty into the aisle where it rolled under a seat and began to rock back and forth in time with the rhythms of the train's movement.

Longarm tilted his head back against the seat cushion and closed his eyes. He wanted to go to sleep, but the movement of the car seemed to be growing.

He groaned out loud and felt an insistent, unwelcome pressure at the back of his throat as the last few drinks tried to push their way back out again.

"Oh, hell," he mumbled. His eyes snapped back open, and he willed the feeling away, concentrating intently on the task of holding his whiskey.

This wasn't *like* him, damn it.

Dimly, distantly, he knew that. But he did not know what to do about it. Or even if he wanted to do anything.

For just a moment there he thought how very nice it would be to crawl off into a corner of the jolting rail car, crawl off into a *dark* corner. Just curl up there and close his

20

eyes and let the movement of the coach lull him off into a long, *long* sleep.

His eyes drooped closed and this time there was no rising gorge to disturb him.

Softly, as if from a far but unimportant distance, he could hear movement in the car nearby and a murmuring of men's voices.

He didn't care.

Right at that moment Deputy U.S. Marshal Custis Long did not really care about a whole hell of a lot.

Then he passed out and cared about nothing at all.

Chapter 4

Longarm felt like someone was pounding his head with sticks. Big sticks. He rather wished, whoever his tormentors were, that they would go ahead and kill him and get it over with. It did not help at all when he opened his eyes and discovered that he was alone.

Moreover, he was alone in a strange room, and he had absolutely no recollection of how he had gotten there. Or of just where "there" was.

Oh, Lordy!

The pounding in his head continued, and he would have hoped for the relief of being able to puke except that his sense of smell told him that he had obviously already managed that. And it was just as obvious that it hadn't helped a bit.

"Oh, Lordy," he repeated, aloud this time.

He sat up—a mistake—and discovered he was in a small, windowless room, lying on a canvas cot that was bare of linen or blankets. The room had a straw-littered earthen floor and no amenities except a slop bucket placed beside the cot. The bucket had been used, but he could not think who might have held his head to help him use the thing. Certainly he had been in no shape to manage that task on his own.

After several unpleasant moments it occurred to him that his unknown benefactor had also taken the trouble to strip his clothes. He was wearing only his balbriggans—and they smelled like they could stand some attention too.

He hadn't been robbed, though. Now that he was looking he could see that his carpetbag was stashed under the head of the cot, and his gunbelt was neatly rolled around his holstered Colt and had been placed on top of the bag.

Longarm shook his head in puzzlement, then winced from the resulting pain the slight motion caused.

This kind of loss of control simply was not *like* him.

He belched, the released belly gases tasting of whiskey and vomit, and thought hard, trying to figure out how much time could have passed—and what the hell might have happened—since his last conscious memories.

Nothing would come. Not a damned thing.

He shuddered, belched again, and wondered if a cheroot would take some of the vile taste out of his mouth. Probably not. He decided against risking it. Hell, shaky as he was feeling right now, he would likely just set himself afire, anyhow. And whoever owned this place where he was didn't deserve *that* form of repayment.

Feeling so weak he was damn near limp, he tried to stand, then thought better of it and settled for swinging his legs off the side of the cot so that he was at least into a mostly upright sitting position. Under the circumstances it could be considered an accomplishment. His head felt like it would split in two separate halves at any sudden motion.

"Oh, boy," he groaned.

This was one hell of a pass for a grown human being to come to. The fact that he was supposed to be a *responsible* grown human being just seemed to make it all the worse.

Disjointed snatches of memory flickered somewhere be-

24

neath the surface of his thoughts.

There was something about leaving the train. Being thrown off it? He didn't know. But he could dimly remember something about winding up face down on the cinders and gravel beside a railroad car. And his bag being there on the ground beside him. He had an idea that he just might have been thrown off the car by some angry passenger, but if that was so he did not particularly want to pursue the memory right now.

Then there was something else about a bottle. Must have been a fresh bottle because he was fairly sure he had killed the jug of Maryland rye he normally carried in his bag. He thought he had done that while he was still on the damned train. But he suspected there had been another one after.

And now. . .?

He couldn't remember a damned thing beyond that.

He shuddered once, felt a rising, insistent pressure deep in his throat, resisted the impulse for only a moment, and then very nearly waited too long. He had to make a dive for the slop bucket to keep from making his current situation even more uncomfortable than it already was.

No one in the history of mankind had ever felt sicker than Custis Long did right at that moment. He was convinced that that was so. No one. Ever.

After a few minutes he tried sitting upright again, then made a monumental effort and actually stood. He swayed like a sapling in a high wind and began to become dizzy. He hadn't balance enough to be sure of keeping his feet, so he dropped abruptly back onto the cot, emitting a loud groan as he did so.

"Son of a bitch," he groaned.

"Feeling better, are you?"

Longarm looked up in genuine horror. The voice was that of a woman.

She had entered the room through a door set right straight in front of him without him ever being aware that she was there until it was too late.

"I'm . . . I'm sorry." He had come to a sorry pass indeed, but that was no excuse for such language in the presence of a lady.

Any lady, much less a young and attractive one like this.

Belatedly it occurred to him that while he was sitting there worrying about his language . . . he was also sitting there in the least of smallclothes.

With a groan that was only partially attributable to the aching in his head, Deputy U.S. Marshal Custis Long pulled his bare legs up and tried to curl himself into a ball on the surface of the blanketless, sheetless cot. He had nothing to cover himself with but embarrassment. And that was not enough to satisfy the bounds of propriety.

Through burning, blood-red ears Longarm could hear the soft, musical sound of the girl's laughter.

"Really," she said. "It isn't all *that* bad."

"Go away? Please?"

"Oh, all right." She had some trouble getting the words out, because she was still laughing at his embarrassment so. "I only came to check on you and to return your clothes. I thought they really needed cleaning."

"Thank you," he mumbled toward the wall, refusing to face her in his current state.

"I'm putting them down by the door here. Are you going to be all right?"

He nodded, even though he was not at all sure that his answer was the truth.

"All right, then. Come out as soon as you are dressed."

Longarm nodded again soundlessly.

"Don't be long," the girl warned. Then with a laugh she added, "Or I'll have to come back and check on you again."

As soon as he heard the door close behind her, Longarm got up. He moved a bit too quickly, swayed dizzily for a moment, but managed to catch himself and walk a shaky course to the freshly washed and pressed clothing that had been laid in a neat pile beside the door. Even his tweed coat and Stetson had been wiped off and carefully brushed. If he had gone and gotten the hat dirty, then he must have been in one helluva shape.

But then, he already knew that from the way he felt.

Still, the movement seemed to be doing him some good. He still felt like he was halfway to the grave, but now he was not so positive that that was where he wanted to be.

He dressed—more with care than with speed—and pulled the door open.

The room where he had spent the night seemed to be part of a storage building originally constructed as a barn but now housing several long, wide-topped tables, each of which had racks built at the ends and along the sides of the tables. He had no idea what the tables were for, but obviously they had been built to some peculiar plan or purpose.

The cheeky damned girl—he could think of her in more normal terms now that he had regained some measure of dignity along with his clothes—was at the back of the huge, barnlike main room rummaging in several cabinets that were attached to the back wall.

She smiled when she saw him. It hurt his pride some when he saw that her smile was not really of welcome but of indulgence. But hell, how seriously could a man expect to be taken when the first impression he made was that of a puking drunk.

"Better?" he asked.

She covered another smile behind a hand, as if remembering her manners now, and nodded.

"Would you mind telling me where I am?" he asked.

"You don't *know?*" She started to laugh again.

"I really don't know," Longarm admitted ruefully.

"Oh, dear. You were worse than I thought."

Longarm stiffened. She might think this was funny, but he didn't. Not a little bit. He drew himself up to his full, considerable height, thought about a biting retort before he got the hell out of her hair, and then realized he hadn't any right to that. Silently he turned back into the smaller room to retrieve his carpetbag.

When he returned to the doorway with it, she was there blocking his exit.

"I didn't mean to insult you," she said softly. "It was just funny. That's all."

Standing in front of her like that, upright and dressed and close for the first time, it occurred to him that she really was damned attractive.

She was fairly tall, at least five-eight, and more willowy than voluptuous. She had wheat-colored hair that was tucked into a smooth roll behind a slender neck. Her eyes were a pale, clear gray. He guessed her age to be somewhere in her late twenties perhaps. More than outward appearance, nice though that was, she had a certain elegance of carriage, a bearing about her that said she was something more than average. A cameo suspended at her throat on a ribbon was not as lovely as the woman who wore it. Longarm felt the return of heat to his cheeks as he realized how he must have seemed to her last night.

She must have noticed his blush, but pretended not to. "I did not answer your question, did I? My apologies, please. You are in Washington."

"Washington? Oh, my God. How'd I get all the way back here?" he blurted.

The District of Columbia was *days* east by the best of rail connections. Surely he couldn't have been drunk all that long without remembering any of it now.

He gave some thought to the queasiness in his belly and decided he was not so sure about that after all.

But if he had taken a train all the way back to Washington . . . What the hell for? He couldn't remember any reason for that. Unless maybe he had decided to turn in his resignation direct to the Attorney General's office rather than face Billy.

If he was going to resign, well, maybe that wouldn't be such a bad idea at that.

Or . . . wait a minute here. He'd been on a *westbound* Union Pacific coach. Maybe he'd stayed on the thing west instead of turning back east. Could be he'd wound up somehow in the other Washington.

Awkwardly he said, "Look, uh, Miss . . . This is rather awkward. If you know what I mean . . ."

28

The girl's facial expression did not change, but there was something in her eyes now that said she was enjoying his embarrassment. "Yes?" she prompted.

"What I, what I wanted to ask was . . . well, *which* Washington would this one be?"

She tried to hide it. Tried to hide it behind steepled fingertips. Gnawed at her lip. Closed her eyes. She just couldn't do it. A giggle escaped her despite her very best efforts to remain serious with him.

"Oh, my. You are in a terrible pickle, aren't you?"

"Yes, ma'am," Longarm agreed with heartfelt sincerity.

The laughter became open now. She tilted her head back to look at him the better, and there were delightful laugh lines around those large gray eyes. He could see, though, that she was not really making fun of him. She was just genuinely amused by his predicament. "You are in Washington, Nebraska," she said and giggled again, hinting that part of his confusion had been deliberately caused by an incomplete answer.

"Washington, Nebraska? Where the—I mean, I never heard of any Washington, Nebraska."

"That may be so, sir, but you found it nonetheless. Or it found you. When you stumbled in here last night you were saying something about some blankety-blank trainmen who wouldn't take you where you wanted to go. I got the impression that you had not wanted to leave the train, you see."

Longarm blushed again. "You say I . . . did I force my way in or something? I hope I wasn't as rude as you must think I am, ma'am."

She giggled again. "Actually, sir, you were quite gallant." She put the accent on the second syllable of the word. "You seemed convinced that your horse was in my 'barn,' you see, and you were determined to ride back to Omaha. Something about seeing a certain lady, I understood."

Longarm had eaten meals that weren't served as hot as his ears felt just then. He tried to stammer an apology.

"Really, it wasn't that bad," she assured him. "As I said,

you were truly gallant. Taken by the liquor, of course, but a gentleman to the end. And I suppose I should pretend to have been horribly shocked and all that, but I was raised with older brothers, sir. You were *much* less troublesome than they used to be." She laughed again, obviously enjoying his discomfort.

Longarm spent several long moments offering apologies, although she seemed to feel that none were necessary. "I don't even recall your name, miss," he finally admitted.

"Sara," she said quickly. "Sara Lewis Hosmer. And you are . . .?"

Longarm colored again. He hadn't even been in control of his senses enough to introduce himself. "Long, Mrs. Hosmer. Custis Long." He opened his mouth to add the title, then stopped short of that.

Identifying himself now as a deputy United States marshal would only be an embarrassment to Billy Vail's office.

Besides, Custis Long was not so sure that he intended to remain a deputy marshal. His behavior of late certainly was no recommendation for the job.

It would serve no purpose to mention it at this point, certainly.

"Of Denver," he added to cover the pause.

"I see," Sara Hosmer said. She smiled. "Well, Mr. Long of Denver, experience with my brothers tells me that the offer of a large breakfast would *not* be wise. But frankly, sir, I haven't had my own breakfast yet. And some weak tea and dry toast might help settle your stomach. Would you join me?"

"You are very kind, Mrs. Hosmer." He smiled. "And very wise. Thank you."

He put his bag down inside the wide front doors of the converted barn and let her lead him across a weedy, grassless yard to the back door of a small house. The bright sunshine outdoors was hell on bloodshot eyes, but he offered no complaint. He was just hoping that Mr. Hosmer would not be too upset when the man saw what the missus was dragging in to the family table so early in the morning.

30

Chapter 5

Sara Hosmer's kitchen was tidy and efficient with a hand pump installed beside a copper sink, an entirely modern design that probably drew water from the cistern Longarm had noticed at the back of the small house on their way inside. There was already a fire crackling in the range, and a tea kettle was leaking steam through its spout.

The woman pointed Longarm toward a seat at the oak table in the middle of the room and said, "This will only take a moment."

"Thanks." Longarm was grateful for the chair. His equilibrium was not all it might have been this morning.

She quickly put tea leaves into a porcelain pot, poured in the boiling water, and covered the pot with a quilted cozy so the tea could steep while she sliced bread and made toast in the oven. Longarm would really have preferred coffee to the tea she was offering, but he was in no position to complain.

When the light meal was served, the toast dry but seeming to help settle the queasiness in his belly, she ate as lightly as he did.

"I'm sorry I can't give you any jam or butter, Mr. Long, but I seem to be out of nearly everything at the moment."

"No problem, ma'am. Is . . . is your husband at work?"

"My husband is dead, Mr. Long. He died in a railroad accident six months ago." She said it with such a blank lack of emotion that he suspected that she was trying to hide a deep grief not from him but from herself. As if by pretending not to feel she could in truth feel nothing of the loss.

He nodded. "This is a difficult time for you, then. My apologies for intruding so rudely, ma'am."

She took another sip of her tea, then looked at him closely. "I just realized something. You are the first person . . . I mean, everyone talks about how awful it was for Roy to have died so young and how sorry they are about it . . . always the same platitudes. I just . . . thank you for not saying the same old things."

"Those same old things are well-intentioned, you know. People, me included, mostly say what they think they ought to, because they know there's nothing they can say or do that will make things right. Mostly I believe they would if they could, though."

She smiled. "I know that. But of course you are right. And I really have gotten over it now."

"Sure," he said, although he didn't believe that for a moment.

Finished, he carried his cup and plate to the copper sink and set them down inside it, then turned and reached for his hat. He was feeling much better now than he had.

"Will you be staying in Washington, Mr. Long?"

He grinned at her. "I hadn't actually intended to come here, you know. I'd never heard of it until you mentioned the name. Now that I'm here," he shrugged, "I might. I have some thinking I need to do. Here might be as good as anyplace to do that."

"Deciding if you want to change jobs," she said.

"How did you . . .?"

"Last night," she explained. "You were rather badly in your cups, you know. You talked about resigning. And you . . ." She shook her head. "Never mind."

He wondered what she had decided at the last moment to leave out, but did not press her on it. Hell, it probably wasn't anything he wanted to hear about anyway.

"What I was wondering," she went on, "was if you would be needing a room. There is a hotel, of course, but . . ."

He began to understand. When she'd taken the can of tea leaves from the pantry he had noticed there was almighty little else in there. With her husband dead and perhaps little or no income now, she would be needing money. A boarder could well be welcome here if he had money to pay.

"Tell you what," he said, "I want to walk around a little anyway." He smiled. "And I certainly haven't anywhere else to go right now. Let me think about it."

"You can leave your things in the shop if you like."

He raised an eyebrow.

"Where you stayed last night. It used to be a barn, but I'm converting it to a shop. I haven't many talents, but I do have a small flair for fashion, I think. And if I can copy designs from the Eastern magazines, perhaps even improve on them a little, I was thinking I might be able to manufacture ladies' clothing here and find a market in Denver."

Which, he realized, might be another part of the reason she would want him to take a room with her. He had said he was from Denver. She might well be hoping he could arrange some useful contacts for her there.

A tight smile tugged at the corners of his lips. Hell, maybe that was just the ticket he needed too. Maybe instead of being a deputy he should go into sales. He could peddle ladies' finery for a living.

"Did I say something funny, Mr. Long?"

"What? Oh. Not at all, ma'am. I was woolgathering.

33

Sorry." He touched the brim of his Stetson. "I'll accept your offer to leave my things where they are then, ma'am, and be back after a while."

"Fine." She went to the sink and began washing up the few dishes she had soiled for their breakfast.

Washington was a typical railside town along the U.P. tracks. It probably developed initially as a short-lived camp for track crews when the line was being built and continued a precarious existence based on an economy of small farms and dairies close to the rails and ranches on the grasslands to the north and south.

There had been a boom of stock-raising in the Nebraska country a few years earlier, and now the farmers were moving in also. Longarm knew that much, even though he had no idea of where Washington would be located between Omaha at one end and Julesburg at the other. Somewhere between them. That was as close as he could be sure.

Wherever the town was, the country around it was uninspiring.

Unlike Denver with its familiar mountains soaring skyward to the west, Washington was surrounded by deceptively rolling land that appeared almost flat at first glance but with countless shallow swales and broad draws crisscrossing the surface in a seemingly haphazard pattern. The country was treeless and windswept. Close to the town the native grasses had been plowed under to make way for field plots of wheat or oats or barley. Windmills were the predominant features beyond the town limits.

The town itself was small but laid out in an orderly pattern, its business district strung along one side of the rails, the opposite side a maze of cattle pens and loading chutes.

Houses, a few of them flanked by struggling windbreak plantings but little ornamentation, were ranked along neatly squared street blocks on three sides of the business district.

Longarm avoided the saloons at the near end of town.

He was feeling better, but his stomach would not suffer that form of abuse again so soon without protest. He walked along the board sidewalks until he reached the hotel that had been built opposite the U.P. depot. The town was too small to have a Harvey House, so he went into the lobby in search of a cup of coffee. Sara Hosmer's tea had been all right, but not exactly satisfying.

There was, he realized, no reason at all for him to stay here. But there was no reason for him to go anywhere else either.

That thought was a disquieting one.

It made him feel alone for the first time he could remember. Alone and without purpose.

He ordered coffee in the hotel's restaurant and drank it without pleasure.

No, damn it, he just wouldn't do it, Longarm decided finally.

Oh, there were temptations enough. Sara Hosmer was an attractive woman. Young and pretty and no doubt vulnerable with her husband dead and her prospects for the future so uncertain.

But she would likely be wanting him to help her with business contacts in Denver and be afraid to offend him by saying no if or when he made a pass at her. There'd never be any way he could know for certain if she was responding to him or was just plain scared of giving offense. A thing like that would be akin to stopping by the killing floor of a slaughterhouse and calling it a hunting trip.

Besides, Longarm admitted to himself with a deep sigh, right at this moment he just didn't want to get involved in anything, with anybody, for any reason whatsoever.

Right now he just wanted . . . Shit, he didn't know *what* he wanted.

Anything. Nothing. It hardly seemed to matter.

Maybe the best thing would just be to go over to the depot and wait for the next train west.

Go back to Denver.

Write out a resignation.

Turn in his badge and wrap the so often used Colt .44 in an oilcloth. Put the thing away in the bottom of a box someplace and . . .

He had no idea what would come after that.

At the moment he truly did not care.

At the moment it hardly seemed to matter.

He was just plain tired of it all.

At the moment that inward weariness of the soul over-shadowed all the rest.

No job; no involvement; no duty; no having to deal constantly with greedy, self-serving assholes; most of all, no having to think about kids lying in comas and maybe dying and the men who made them that way whining and sniveling and going unharmed to a warm jail cell.

Maybe the best damn thing would just be to turn in that resignation and crawl off in a corner someplace.

It wouldn't hardly matter what corner he crawled into. Just so it was one where Custis Long, *Mister* Custis Long, thank you, private citizen, didn't have to be involved in all the miseries of mankind.

He could get along. He always had. It wouldn't matter what he was doing to get along.

Wouldn't matter a lick.

Not to anybody. Himself included.

He belched, and a wry smile twisted at the corners of his lips. Judging from the way his stomach still felt this morning, his future didn't lie as a drunk, anyhow. He'd have to write off that possibility.

The thing to do, he figured, would be to stop across the street at the U.P. depot and check the schedule for the next westbound. Then go back to Sara Hosmer's place. Tell her he wouldn't be staying and collect his things from her workshop. Then just sit quietly and wait for the train to carry him back to Denver so he could turn in his badge.

Yeah, he thought. Why not.

He finished his coffee and dropped a nickel beside the cup to pay for it, pushed back away from the table, and made his way slowly out into the sunshine.

Funny, he thought, how old and slow he was feeling all

36

of a sudden. He moved and felt like a man twice his age. And the truth was that he observed this in himself without giving a particular shit about it.

The station was just across the street from the hotel. There was no street traffic to watch out for. Likely the town of Washington would be busy in the evenings and busier on the weekends, but right now it was almost empty. The farmers and ranchers from the surrounding country would be off at their labors instead of lazing around town. During the workdays the place was nearly deserted. That suited Longarm just find.

He noticed that a train was stopped on the rails now, taking on water from the high, wooden tank tower. He was not really interested in it, though, and made no effort to hurry. The short freight was pointed east and did not concern him.

He moved slowly forward, drawn so deep within himself and his own miseries that he barely noticed when a ragged burst of gunfire erupted from somewhere on the other side of the Union Pacific depot.

Chapter 6

Longarm's lethargy was so great that he stood rooted where he was, watching, as more gunfire sounded from behind the depot. Moments later there was the sound of gunfire from a block or two east, somewhere in the business district of the town.

Something . . . it wasn't his *business*, damn it . . . was going on.

There were very few people on the street. Of the few there were, several began running. Others ducked out of sight.

Down at the water tank the train whistle shrilled, and the engineer threw power to the driving wheels, lurching the train forward while the dump pipe from the tank remained down, its flimsy nozzle tucked within the filler tube on top of the engine's boiler. The movement of the train caught the water tender by surprise, breaking off part of the filler pipe and dumping a rush of water over the engine cab and coal car as the train shifted forward. The crewman, probably the fireman, who had been standing atop the boiler lost his grip on the filler chain and was knocked off his feet. The man fell heavily to the gravel and cinder side of the roadbed and screamed in pain. From the top of the engine to the ground was a drop of a dozen feet or more, and his leg was twisted at an unnatural angle.

The shooting near the depot stopped almost at once when the train moved, and moments later Longarm could hear hoofbeats along the far side of the train.

Within seconds a small group of horsemen swept around the front of the train, their horses outpacing the movement of the train as they raced around the front of the engine, leaping the tracks and into sight.

One of the men—there were three of them—turned in his saddle to snap a shot toward the engineer, who was protected by the steel walls of the cab.

The horsemen raced into the street and down it to the east.

A puff of gunsmoke appeared from a doorway in the next block, and all three horsemen returned the fire, shooting point blank into the doorway as they raced past.

A man's body toppled forward onto the sidewalk from the shadows of the doorway.

Belatedly, Longarm palmed his Colt, although the distance was impossibly long for a handgun. He no longer thought of himself as a deputy marshal but, damn it, he could not stand by and idly watch something like this.

He fired twice, missing each time. The horsemen were so far away now that none of them bothered to shoot back at him.

As the men raced into the next block, three more horses swept out of an alley toward them.

For a moment Longarm thought the newcomers might be townspeople or local cowboys happening by who were in time to intercept the gang.

Instead this second trio of riders, each of them brandishing upraised revolvers, swung into close formation be-

40

hind the first bunch, joining them in their flight from town.

Someone stepped out of a building far up the street but was quickly driven back inside by the discharge of six revolvers in the hapless man's direction.

Off to the right the train whistle shrieked in futile protest as the six gang members leaned low over their horses' necks and spurred the animals into a hard run for freedom.

Six men, Longarm thought with quick, professional appraisal, divided to hit two separate targets in one swift, bold raid and then away. One target a car, presumably the baggage or mail car, of the train while it was stopped to take on water. The other, one of the businesses several blocks away. Then the planned getaway, made together for the safety of numbers. That engineer having the wit to jump the train forward would have worried them. It could have temporarily cut off their planned line of escape.

The horsemen reached the end of the business district and wheeled their horses into a hard left turn, revolvers still held at the ready, as they raced out of sight onto one of the residential streets of the town.

To the north lay countless miles of unfenced grasslands where they could lose themselves in the swales and gullies of the featureless, rolling countryside.

Unless, of course, someone was damned quick about getting on their trail.

Automatically, from long habit, Longarm reloaded his .44 before he shoved it back into his holster.

Someone would have to. But not him, damn it. This was *not* his responsibility.

Even if he hadn't yet had a chance to officially and formally turn in his resignation, robberies were local problems to be handled by local peace officers.

This one was *not* Custis Long's affair.

Men, most of them storekeepers in shirtsleeves and sleeve garters, were beginning to appear on the street now that the dust of the gang's getaway was settling.

Some of the men were waving rifles and shotguns with confused enthusiasm, even though there was nothing left for them to shoot at.

Others were asking excited questions in loud voices but not taking the time to listen for rational answers.

Amateurs, Longarm thought with the detachment of a spectator's disinterest.

A crowd of shouting, gabbling townspeople was beginning to assemble in the street a block away. Off to the right of them the train had been brought to a halt again and was backing toward the station and the workman who continued to lie at the side of the roadbed with his broken leg.

Longarm drifted toward the assembly, even though this was none of his affair. His only thought at the moment was that this robbery business might delay the departure of the eastbound train and cause a rescheduling of the westbound he intended to take back to Denver.

Still, he had nothing better to do right now. He might as well stand around there as anywhere else.

"Ruined," a florid, aging man with more gray than dark in his beard was wailing. "We're ruined. They got . . . they took everything. Everything."

The sign over the door of the building he had come from—the same place the robbers had just visited—said Bank of Washington in large, gold-colored lettering.

"What d'you mean everything?" demanded a man in sleeve garters.

"You heard me, Henry. Everything. Cash . . . we brought cash in. Special all the way from Chicago. To loan to John Holbert so he could buy a herd of stockers being brought up from Texas. It would've been a good loan, Henry. No risk to the depositors with the cattle for collateral. It would've been a good loan." The words came out in a quavering voice.

"But that doesn't have anything t'do with us, right? I mean, our money's safe. You're covered by insurance, aren't you, Jace?"

The banker, Jace, wrung his hands and refused to look any of the other men in the eye.

"Well?" the storekeeper demanded.

Jace gulped for air like a fish thrown onto a creek bank. "I . . . the insurance only covers to a few thousand dollars,

Henry. We never keep much cash on hand. Everybody knows that. We never have much actual cash on hand. No need for more insurance than that."

"Except for this time?"

Miserable and sweating heavily now, the banker nodded. "Except for just right now."

"How much did they get?" someone else asked.

It took Jace a few moments to get the words out. "Forty . . . forty-two thousand. Everything."

"My God," someone blurted. "That could near wipe out the whole town. All of us ruined."

"Lordy, Lordy," somebody else put in. "And those sons o' bitches hit the baggage car for a gold shipment too. No telling what they got away with there."

"The hell with somebody else's gold," a more practical townsman said. "We got to get our money back."

"Where's Harlan?" another voice asked.

"The hell with Harlan! Where's Ron Deal?"

The names, of course, meant nothing to Longarm, but that was sorted out a moment later when two more men appeared, making their way up the street from the direction of the hotel. Longarm recalled having seen the two of them there while he was having his coffee.

One was heavyset and probably in his fifties, the other a younger and much trimmer man. Both wore revolvers and both had officious, grim looks about them. It turned out that the older man was Harlan Walker, sheriff for whatever county Washington was in, while the young man was town marshal Ron Deal. Deal's arrival to join the group was slowed by the ponderously deliberate gait adopted by the sheriff.

Longarm stood silently observing and listening while the once again excited and now nearly distraught townspeople tried to fill the local lawmen in on what had happened, their efforts hampered by the fact that everyone was trying to tell the story at once.

Finally Deal took charge by bellowing for silence, then pointing out one man at a time to tell the tale, starting with the banker. After that things went a little better.

The bank had been robbed. Simultaneously the train had been robbed. A man called Ig was dead and at least four others had been wounded or otherwise injured in the twin robberies.

And of course the holdup gang was long since gone and away with their considerable profits from a short day's work.

Deal collected the facts efficiently, then turned to the sheriff, waiting for the older man to take charge.

Sheriff Walker cleared his throat and glared from one man to the next in the crowd, as if the whole thing was somehow their fault. "Well," he said finally, "there ain't much to it but that we got to chase those sons o' bitches down and get that money back. Wouldn't you say so, Ron?"

Marshal Deal nodded.

"I'll be taking charge of the posse, o' course, but I'd like you to ride along if you would, Ron," the sheriff said.

"Of course. Whatever you need."

"And I'll be needing some volunteers for the posse," the sheriff added.

A good many of the men in the crowd seemed suddenly less interested in the proceedings than they had been. These were, Longarm reminded himself, townspeople, not gunhands or even cowboys. They were mostly men who expected the comforts of a soft mattress and a well-laid table.

"No volunteers?" Deal snapped.

"I'll go," someone said, although he sounded reluctant about it.

"Me too." Both of the volunteers were young men probably in their early twenties.

"Charlie?" Deal asked.

The man who responded to that question did not look happy, but after a moment's hesitation he nodded.

"We need more than that, boys," the sheriff prompted.

But no one else was eager to chase after a group of six armed and dangerous robbers.

"Harlan is too polite to remind you, boys, but I'm not,"

44

the marshal put in. "The thing is, he has the authority to commandeer posse members or whatever else he needs." Longarm got the impression that Deal wasn't so much reminding the men of that as making a pointed reminder to the sheriff. "Anybody he says rides, rides. Or goes to jail for refusing. Those are the choices."

There was some grumbling about that, and a few of the men—probably those who had little or nothing on deposit at the bank anyway—began to sidle away from the gathering as unobtrusively as they could.

"I want you to come, and you," Sheriff Walker said, pointing.

One of the new possemen sighed, then nodded. The other shook his head. "Now damn it, Harlan, you know my missus ain't feeling good. She's been sick for days now. What'd happen to my business if I have to close it down and go off waving a gun in the air? Take this fella. He can handle a gun better'n me anyhow. I seen him shoot at them robbers while they was running. He'd do you more good than I ever could."

Longarm blinked. The silly son of a bitch was pointing at *him*.

"But . . ."

"I didn't know Mayva was sick, Jesse. I'm sorry to hear that," the sheriff said. He turned and eyed Longarm. "You'll do, son."

"Now, wait a minute. I've got business in Denver. I can't—"

"The sheriff says you can," Marshal Deal said. "So I expect you can. Either that or sit in my jail waiting for the circuit judge to get here. And there's no telling how long that will be. Quite a spell, maybe."

"I don't have a horse to ride, or . . ."

"I'll give you the borry of one," the man called Jesse put in quickly. "Got a real good horse you can use."

Sheriff Walker nodded briskly, accepting Longarm's inclusion in the posse as an accomplished fact now. He pointed to two more men and informed them that they would be riding with the group too. Each of them glanced

45

not at the sheriff but at the town marshal, then nodded a resigned acceptance of the order.

"Good," Walker said with satisfaction. "I'll give you boys fifteen minutes to get ready. Get your horses and guns and meet me back here right on this spot, ready to ride. Lenny, while they're doing that I want you to make up some pokes of food for us to be carrying along."

"What about . . ."

Walker held a hand up to stop the question. "You mark down what you put up for us. The county will pay for it, or Jace will. We'll work that out when we get back with the stolen money and those murdering sons o' bitches that took it."

"All right, Sheriff."

"And, Jesse," the sheriff added, "don't you forget to bring your horse around for this young feller t' use. Can't go off chasing a pack of desperadoes afoot."

The sheriff chuckled.

Hell, he was acting like those "desperadoes" of his were already as good as in irons.

Longarm rolled his eyes, but said nothing. What the hell had he gone and gotten himself into here?

"Off y' go now. Meet back here in fifteen minutes."

Longarm turned, intending to head back toward Sara Hosmer's house, where his saddle and rifle were. Marshal Deal stopped him with a light touch on the elbow.

"We'll be seeing you here in fifteen minutes, mister. Right?"

Longarm hesitated only for a moment. Then he nodded. "I'll be here."

Deal smiled, but there was neither humor nor friendliness in the expression.

"If it helps any," the town marshal said, "the county pays seventy-five cents a day for posse duty."

"Thanks," Longarm drawled bitterly.

It wasn't turning out to be so easy to get shut of law enforcing, he thought as he moped his way back down toward the other end of the town.

Chapter 7

They were a helluva posse, Longarm decided as he
watched Sheriff Harlan Walker's possemen assemble. He
sat on his borrowed horse—a "real good one," had that
idiot called it? Poor bastard obviously didn't know horseflesh from horseflies.

Of the eight men who would be going after the holdup
gang, only Longarm and Marshal Deal looked like they
halfway knew what they were doing.

For sure, the good sheriff of whatever this county was
did not act like he was accustomed to such work. In fact,
he looked distinctly uncomfortable on the back of a horse
he had borrowed from Ron Deal.

The two young townsmen at least looked like they were
willing to give the job their best effort. They were decently
mounted and had revolvers strapped at their waists. Two of
the other possemen were armed only with double-barreled

scatterguns, and one man was carrying a decrepit Spencer repeater that would serve as a dandy bludgeon, but not much else.

The man named Lenny handed out small parcels of food for each man to tie behind his saddle. Longarm did not bother to look inside the sack he was given, but several of the townsmen did. There was a short round of bitching about having to go off with nothing but hardtack and cheese until Sheriff Walker hushed them with a reminder that with luck they might be back for supper by nightfall.

"Bring them back, boys, and the bank will stand treat for steaks and all the liquor you can hold," the banker added. That offer brought a revival of interest to the group. At the moment, though, his stomach still doing flip-flops after his recent stupidity, Longarm failed to be excited by the prospect.

Besides, the holdup gang by now had the better part of an hour's start on the posse, and unless Harlan Walker was a hell of a lot better tracker than he was an organizer, it would surprise Long to see anyone wearing handcuffs before nightfall.

"Ready, men?" the sheriff called out.

It looked like they were until one of the conscripts from the town dropped his poke of food and they all had to wait while he dismounted and tried to rebundle everything and tie it behind his cantle. Walker cussed some over that delay. Ron Deal sat on his leggy, well-made roan, trying not to look amused. Longarm probably would have agreed with the marshal if he hadn't been feeling so damned annoyed himself.

Finally, at least half an hour after Walker announced they would be leaving in fifteen minutes, everyone seemed ready to go.

"All right, men. Follow me," Walker shouted. He dug his boot heels into the sides of his horse and sent the startled animal into a slow gallop out of town in the direction the gang had not too recently taken.

Skeptical as hell but not seeming to have all that much choice about it, Longarm followed along with the others.

Ron Deal, he noticed, was loping along easily at the back of the procession.

Longarm almost shuddered when he realized that behind them the banker and some of the other townspeople were sending them off with waving hats and a hearty round of "Hip, hip, hurrah, boys! Hip, hip, hurrah!"

Harlan Walker on horseback was a genuinely imposing figure of a man. Big, beefy, and riding stiffly upright, he would have looked grand in a parade. No doubt his grandiose carriage and bearing had something to do with his ability to be elected to public office.

On the other hand, Longarm strongly suspected the man had little actual field experience when it came to tracking down criminals.

Longarm knew damned good and well, because he had stood in the street and observed the whole robbery and subsequent organization of the posse, that no one had seen for sure just which way the robber gang went after they swept out of sight around that street corner.

Yet Walker did not lower himself to asking questions of the common folks who might actually have seen the escape from town.

The posse rode past a dozen homes the raiders must have passed in their flight, and in several of the yards around those homes there were children who must surely have observed the gang racing past. In one back yard a plump, matronly woman was busy hanging her morning's washing out to dry. She surely would have seen the gang. Probably even got pissed with them for raising a dust near her newly washed clothes.

Walker led his posse right on by, as if he could not stoop to asking questions of those without authority.

Maybe he wasn't being particularly charitable here, Longarm conceded, but his opinion was that it never hurt to learn a little something. The good sheriff either disagreed with that viewpoint or simply never thought to ask.

Whatever, Custis Long was not going to try to take over responsibility for this chase.

He was through with being a peace officer. He would do what he had to do now, ride along with the rest of them until Walker and company got tired of chasing around the countryside, then quietly board the next available train west and turn his resignation in to Billy Vail.

That was all there was to it. That was the end of his responsibility here.

"This way, boys," the sheriff called out authoritatively.

Walker swung his horse toward the northeast as they cleared the last houses of Washington.

The choice was a logical one, even if there were no obvious tracks for them to be following yet, so close to town where the normal traffic of horses and wagons would confuse the issue. The fenced barnyard and pasture of a small dairy farm lay directly ahead of them now, and the sheriff led his men around it before again turning north onto the open range.

Longarm had plenty of doubts about the eventual outcome of this chase, though.

The robbers had nearly an hour's head start on the posse, and sheer speed was not going to catch them, even if Walker was sure he knew what direction the gang would be taking.

Longarm had seen the horses those robbers were riding, and they were superior to every animal in the posse, with the possible exception of Ron Deal's mount. The town marshal, even if his official duties would not take him outside the confines of Washington, seemed to have a good eye for horseflesh. All the other horses were of ordinary quality. The robbers, with something extra at stake when they got into a horse race, had chosen their animals with care.

With Sheriff Walker in the lead, though, the posse jolted forward across the grass at a pace that would be impossible to maintain for long. Longarm quit fretting about it—the choices were not his to make here—and relaxed in his McClellan, taking his weight on the stirrups so the bars of the saddle would ride easiest on the horse's back. Some

50

of the men were already urging their mounts to stay up with the pace set by the sheriff, but Longarm kept his reins slack with his spurs away from his borrowed horse's flanks, letting the animal keep with the rest at the easiest gait possible. A few yards behind Longarm, Marshal Ron Deal was doing the same thing. Gradually a slight gap separated Longarm and Deal from the rest of the group, widening slowly for a time and then almost imperceptibly closing as the horses to the fore began to tire.

After less than an hour, Walker brought them to a halt. His horse was sweat-lathered and breathing heavily, as were several others in the group. Longarm's animal and Deal's mount still had plenty left in reserve.

"Loosen your cinches, boys, and let 'em blow for a minute here," Walker ordered. "Then we'll get after 'em again."

The possemen dismounted and did as they were told, Longarm included.

"We've closed on them, boys. I'm sure of it," Walker announced, although as far as Longarm could see the man had no reason for believing it to be so.

Several of the townsmen who had been impressed into the posse gripped their weapons and looked nervously around after the sheriff's words.

There damn sure was nothing for them to see, though.

Longarm lighted a cheroot, let the reins of his horse drop to the ground, and stepped a few feet away from the horse to have his own look around.

He was only slightly interested in the terrain here, and not at all apprehensive that they were anywhere near the robber gang. Mostly what he wanted to do was to learn now if this unknown animal could be trusted to ground tie. The animal stood where it was, dropping its muzzle to crop at the thick carpet of short browning grass underfoot. That was hardly conclusive, but at least he knew that the horse would not immediately try to bolt for freedom if he turned loose of it.

While he was doing that he was observing the countryside they were passing through.

Here there was no hint that a town could be anywhere around.

The nearest buildings might have been hundreds of miles away for all anyone could see. Or they might, as Longarm knew to be the case, be only a relatively few miles behind.

In this great, virtually treeless grassland, a man could see to the horizon in any direction he chose to look.

The thing was, that horizon might be several miles distant. Or it might as easily be a matter of only a hundred yards away. And sometimes it was damned difficult to tell which distance was the nearer to the truth.

With no objects of known size in sight to give a man a perspective on things, distances were damnably difficult to judge.

The endless folds and rises and swales, every inch of them covered by grass as if carpeted with the stuff, gave no clues to direction or distance or what might lie beyond the next rise.

It was a deceptive country, where a man would think he could see a prairie dog move a mile away—and indeed very well might if the lie of the terrain in that particular spot happened to permit it—yet where a regiment of infantry, or a tribe of hostile Sioux, could pass unnoticed within a quarter mile of the most observant sentry. It was all a matter of contours and happenstance.

"You wouldn't have a light, would you?"

Longarm turned. Marshal Deal was standing beside him with a pencil-thin black cheroot in hand.

"Of course." Instead of wasting a match, Longarm held out his own cheroot so Deal could apply the glowing tip of it to start his smoke.

"Thanks."

"Por nada."

Deal puffed on his cheroot for a moment, seeming to enjoy the taste of it. Behind him the other possemen were gathered close around Walker, who was assuring them that the gang would be in custody and the money returned safely to Washington by nightfall.

"You've done this sort of thing before," Deal said.

Longarm shrugged. It was not a subject he wanted to go into at the moment.

"Comes the time we catch up with them, I'll likely be wanting to count on you," Deal said, pursuing the unwelcome subject despite Longarm's reluctance. Longarm found it interesting, though, that the town marshal was assuming he would have to take some measure of command if Sheriff Walker ever brought them within striking distance of the gang.

That, of course, was questionable itself. Longarm said as much.

Deal disagreed. "There is no place for a man to hide out here, much less half a dozen riders," the marshal said.

Longarm raised an eyebrow and looked around them out toward the deceptively empty grassland. "You could hide an army out there, a whole town, and pass by it never the wiser, unless you got lucky enough to ride onto it."

"You really think so?" Deal asked.

"I do."

The marshal gave Longarm a tight-lipped smile that held no humor. "You say we are wasting our time, then?"

"Not at all. I hope we have that luck, for the sake of all the folks who had their money in that bank."

Deal grunted. "But you don't believe it will happen?"

"I don't believe or disbelieve," Longarm said. "I'll ride. I'll do what I can. I'll hope for the best. But believing or not—mine, yours, anybody's—won't make a lick of difference in the matter."

Deal grunted again without comment, took a deep draw on the cheroot captured between his teeth, and turned back to the rest of the group.

"I say we've closed the gap on them considerable, Ron," Walker said loudly. "What d'you think?"

"I think we still have a ways to go, Sheriff."

"And right you are. We've rested the horses long enough, men. Pull those cinches tight and mount up."

Several of the men, obviously those who had little experience with getting the most out of a horse, yanked their cinches like they were trying to cut their horses in two. Longarm snugged his just enough to allow him to mount, stepped into the saddle, and then reached down to slip the cinch even looser. The freer a horse could breathe, the more it could give you.

He noticed that Ron Deal did not even do that. The Washington town marshal allowed his cinch to hang a good inch under his horse's belly and vaulted lightly into his saddle without using his stirrups.

The man was a horseman, Longarm thought. From Longarm's point of view that was a compliment.

"Right, boys," Sheriff Walker's voice rang loudly with the force of command. "Follow me."

Once again the sheriff spurred his barely cooling horse from a dead stop straight into a gallop.

Chapter 8

"Time to rest the horses again, boys," Sheriff Walker said, not quite so loudly this time.

Actually, Longarm suspected it was not so much the horse that Walker wanted to rest now—although the animal could certainly use it—as the sheriff's own backside. For the past three quarters of an hour or so, the heavyset man, obviously not accustomed to long hours in a saddle and likely more at home in an armchair or seated at a poker table, had been shifting his butt from one cheek to the other and even at times standing in his stirrups to take the weight off his considerable ass. The result of something like that was damned little relief for the rider and a much harder time for the horse.

The posse drew to an obedient halt, most of them looking every bit as relieved as the sheriff to be able once again to dismount and walk around for a few minutes.

The only ones who seemed not to feel the discomfort of the ride were Longarm, Deal, and the two young men who had volunteered to ride with the posse.

Oddly, Longarm thought, the talk at these now frequent rest stops was becoming more forceful as the day wore on, although delivered in softer tones.

"I say we string the sons of bitches up quick as we catch them," a shopkeeper observed to no one in particular.

"Damn right," another man agreed.

It was as if the uncomfortable riders were no longer so interested in the probable failure of the bank for lack of the stolen money and the impact that would have on their town. Now they were feeling a sense of personal vengeance for all the miseries they were suffering.

String 'em up indeed, Longarm thought with wry amusement.

Quite aside from the fact that there wasn't a tree within twenty miles that anyone here seemed to know about, the first chore remained. Kind of like that recipe for making rabbit stew. First you catch the rabbit.

Well, first these fellows were going to have to catch their gang of robbers.

And so far Longarm couldn't see that Sheriff Walker and his posse had a hope in hell of doing that.

The only living creatures Longarm had seen all afternoon other than the posse he rode with had been a handful of cattle grazing on open range and the frequent bands of antelope that bolted out of sight in the distance whenever the party of riders came into view.

Even if Harlan Walker was one hell of a tracker, and so far there had been no indications that he was, this was tough country to trail anyone in.

The thick carpet of grass lay over a base of soft sand that was easily indented but which held only the vaguest of impressions.

It would be impossible here to follow the tracks of a given horse even if the hoofprint was as familiar to the tracker as the contours of his own face in a shaving mirror.

Longarm had paid some attention back in town from

56

force of habit to the tracks of the horses they would be following, but it was not possible to apply that knowledge in the Nebraska sand hills.

With such formless imprints left by the passage of a hoof, it was frequently difficult to tell if a track had been left by a horse or a steer, much less by any particular horse.

Hell, the only way to differentiate between the tracks of a cow and a pronghorn were by the size. Shapes were simply impossible to determine.

So, as far as Longarm could tell, the posse's chances of success were becoming slimmer with every passing hour.

They could be fifty miles apart by now if gang and posse had taken different directions.

On the other hand, the gang could be a quarter of a mile away on the far side of the next rise.

There just was no way to tell.

Still, the men and their elected leader remained convinced that they were within a hairsbreadth of victory.

"We got to be close to them now, Harlan," one of the possemen said, "hard as we've been pushin'."

Longarm somehow managed to keep a straight face. For most of the afternoon, Sheriff Walker had been "resting his horse"—and his butt—a good fifth of the time.

The fellow who had made that statement, though, believed it. Longarm was sure the man was not trying to be sarcastic. He simply knew no better.

"Right, Bradley," the sheriff assured him. "We're close to them now. I c'n feel it."

That was one way to know such things, Longarm supposed. Maybe a better way than most under these circumstances, in fact.

"One thing, boys," the sheriff warned. "Any of those sons of bitches as gets shot trying to avoid capture, that's his bad luck. But we won't be having any necktie parties on any posse of mine. I want you should get that straight, right here an' now. Any of 'em we put in irons go back for a fair an' impartial trial."

There was some grumbling about that, but with no rabbit to put into the stew pot yet the point was moot.

Longarm ground reined his horse, which was still nearly as fresh as when they had departed Washington in the morning, and turned away from the group to light a cheroot and take a leak. He hadn't had anything to eat yet today except for the bit of dry toast Mrs. Hosmer had given him, and his stomach had recovered enough by now that he would be pleased when Walker decided it was time to stop for a meal.

While he was thinking about that, Ron Deal joined him again, unbuttoned his fly to relieve himself on the ground, and then took out a cheroot. Longarm again offered the town marshal a light from the coal of his own smoke.

"Thanks. I should've known enough to bring some matches."

"A man can't think of everything."

"True." Deal puffed with pleasure on his smoke. "I forgot something else today too," he said. "My manners. I'm Ron Deal."

"Custis Long," Longarm said. A week ago he would have added a title and perhaps a nickname to go with that, but today he did not feel that either applied.

Deal offered his hand to shake. In a lower voice he asked, "So what is your opinion now, Mr. Long?"

Again all Longarm would give him was a shrug.

Deal smiled a little. "You're polite, anyway. Are you planning to settle in Washington, Mr. Long?"

"No, just passing through."

"Stopped on business, did you?"

Normally Longarm might have resented the questioning, but he realized that in this case the town marshal was only doing a job that Sheriff Walker had neglected. This man calling himself Custis Long was, after all, an unknown quantity to the people of Washington.

"No," Longarm said. "I'm between jobs right now. I stopped in Washington just by chance." That was pretty much the truth. Certainly as close to it as he wanted to get at the moment. Explanations about the badge Longarm continued to carry in his wallet would only confuse things, and at this point could be an active irritant once the town marshal and county sheriff discovered there was an unannounced federal deputy marshal in the posse.

No, Longarm thought, better not to open *that* particular can of worms. Especially since it was apparent that this posse was not going to gain anything except the benefits of fresh air and exercise.

There would be no harm done by keeping his mouth shut.

Deal puffed on his cheroot and gave Longarm a speculative look, but he was not accusing about it or even unpleasant. Just curious. As he properly should have been.

"Thanks for the light," he said, and returned to the group of townspeople he knew and would continue to live with. Custis Long would be of interest to him no longer than the life of this posse.

Longarm finished his smoke and went to his horse to take some hardtack out of the bag that had been handed to him back in town. He was damn sure hungry, hungry enough that even the rocklike crackers would be welcome.

He smiled a little as he slowly chewed on the first bite, trying to moisten and soften the bland, dry stuff before he swallowed.

No wonder the storekeeper had sent hardtack with the posse. The fellow might have had the things on his shelves unsold since his store was opened. It would be no wonder that he would want to get rid of it at this opportunity to unload it on the county treasury.

It was coming dark, but still Sheriff Harlan Walker had not stopped for supper. He continued to stop frequently on the pretext of resting the horses, but was unwilling to take the time for the possemen to eat. Longarm gave the man unexpected credit. Walker might not know a hell of a lot about chasing criminals on open ground, he might be overweight and tender of ass, but he had his own brand of down-deep tenacity. There was certainly that to be said for him.

By now the other members of the posse were becoming tired and hungry too, and as local voters they could feel freer than Longarm to express opinions about that. One of them bumped his horse into a quicker gait so he could approach the sheriff at the head of their little procession.

"Harlan."

"Uh-huh?"

"It's 'most too dark to track now. Why can't we stop and have us a little somethin' to eat?"

Longarm dropped his head to hide the smile that was tickling the corners of his lips. The man who had asked the question seemed to be under the misinformed notion that their worthy leader was following tracks. There hadn't been any tracks they could really follow ever since they thundered so precipitously away from Washington. And that had been a good many hours ago now.

"Not yet, Jonesy," the sheriff said.

"But we can't—" the man started to protest.

"I know what you're fixing to tell me, Jonesy, an' you're right. Far as it goes. Too dark already to be tracking. But we ain't tracking now. Now we're looking for their firelight."

"We are?"

Walker nodded firmly. "They think they've lost us by now, Jonesy. Bound to be thinkin' that. They can't know we been hanging so close to them. That's our advantage, y'see. They stop an' build a fire, son, then we can spot it an' move right in on 'em."

The sheriff had been talking loud enough for all to hear. His assurances, so full of confidence, caused most of the men to sit straighter in their saddles. A few of the men even went so far as to check their firearms to make sure all was in readiness for a capture Longarm was convinced would never take place.

Longarm glanced to his right, toward where Ron Deal was easily keeping pace and riding not far from Longarm's side. It was the place Deal had chosen to ride through most of the afternoon.

Longarm was not positive in the failing light of dusk, but he thought the town marshal gave him a wink. Of course it could only have been that the marshal had gotten a gnat in his eye about then. But Longarm didn't think so.

"If any of you is all that hungry," Walker said to the group, "you can pull something out of your sacks the next time we stop. But we won't be taking time to make fires or cook anything. This is our best chance, y'see. Got to take advantage of it while we can."

They rode on largely in silence until the sheriff's next rest stop. Then most of the men, Longarm included, took the opportunity to take a cold supper out of their pokes. There was considerable grumbling about the hardtack and a great deal more of it when the men realized that none of them had thought to pack canteens of water. The store-keeper back in Washington had sent a bag of already ground coffee beans in Walker's sack, but no one had thought to bring water to make the coffee. A fire would have been useless without that anyway, as neither the hard-tack nor the cheese needed heating.

The cheese, Longarm reflected as he chewed on some of it, wasn't bad.

But now that everyone had noticed the oversight with the water, everyone insisted on talking about it. It was enough to make Longarm salivate at the thought of a long, chill drink. There was no telling how the others were doing in that regard.

Unfortunately, a few of them made up for the lack of coffee by pulling whiskey bottles out of their saddlebags.

If no one had remembered water, practically no one had neglected to bring a jug of liquor.

Longarm did not particularly like that idea. Posses and alcohol were rarely a good mix, in his experience.

He did not worry about it overmuch, though. Consider-ing the odds against their finding the gang members at this point, probably the only harm from it would be the hang-overs the men would suffer tomorrow.

Having just gotten over a first-class, grade-A rip-snorter of a hangover himself, Longarm refused the one offer of a drink he got and tried to forget about being thirsty.

Long experience had taught him that dwelling on a problem would not make it go away and could only make things seem even worse than they were. So he tried to set

61

aside the dryness in his throat and think about other things.

Like, for instance, the pleasant appearance of Sara Hosmer.

The widow was a handsome woman. And if Longarm was going to be laid over in Washington waiting for the next westbound after they got back to town . . .

"You sure you don't want a drink?" the posse member offered again.

"Thank you, but no."

The man shrugged and tipped his bottle back. Longarm thought his name was Kurt. Something like that. Longarm had not made any particular attempt to get to know the other members of Walker's posse, but he heard names now and then when they were talking among themselves. As an outsider in their midst, conversation was rarely directed his way.

The men ate and drank while their horses rested. Then, on the sheriff's command, they swung back into their saddles and took up a road jog, still trending north and east from distant Washington.

After twenty minutes or so Walker reined to a stop on top of one of the many rises, and the others filtered forward to join him.

Most of them, Longarm noticed, still had bottles in their free hands, although the cheese and hardtack had long since disappeared.

"See!" the sheriff said with satisfaction. "Just what I told you would happen."

The men stood in their stirrups and peered in the direction Walker was pointing.

"Well, I'll be damned," Longarm muttered.

Up ahead, not half a mile away in the gloom of the early, still moonless night, they could all see the faint gleam of a low campfire.

"Just like I said," Walker declared. "Check your guns, boys, an' get ready for whatever comes. We go quiet from here on. Real quiet and all together. When I signal, we all spread out, slow an' easy, an' slip up in a ring around 'em. We don't want any of them gettin' away from us now."

Longarm looked at Deal. The town marshal was frowning.

"C'mon now, boys. Watch for my signal. And don't nobody shoot unless they fire first. We take 'em back for trial if ever we can. You got that?"

Walker looked sternly from one member of the posse to the next, making eye contact with each man in turn and not looking to the next until he had received a nod of a head or a "yes" or some other indication that the instruction had been received and understood.

No one was to fire until or unless it was necessary.

"All right then, boys. Let's go get 'em."

The sheriff moved his horse forward in a slow walk.

Chapter 9

The men from Washington did their very best. And no doubt they really believed they were being quiet. Still, the only members of the posse who bothered—or who knew —to muffle their bit chains and tie their spur rowels were Longarm and Ron Deal. A drum and bugle corps might have been a little louder making that final approach on the "enemy" campfire, Longarm figured. Maybe.

Even so, the men who were bedded down beside the dying fire did not try to bolt away into the night.

As they came near, Sheriff Walker directing the movements of his possemen with broad sweeps of his arms, Longarm could see that there were two bedrolls laid by the fire.

One of the men was sleeping soundly, but as the jangle and thump of approaching hooves and loose equipage came closer, the other man stirred and rolled over under his soogan.

The man stirred some more, yawned, and stretched. One arm flopped out to the side and touched the other man, who was sleeping nearby.

It all looked like a man who was simply shifting position in his sleep and was unaware of the oncoming danger, but Longarm knew better.

The fellow was wide awake, Longarm was sure, and was no doubt scared.

Putting himself in the suddenly awakened fellow's place for a moment, Longarm thought it through. What the man would be hearing. What he might be thinking.

Assuming he was not one of the Washington bank robbers—and with only two men in this camp there was no reason in the world to think that these two were members of the gang—the man would be coming out of a sound sleep to find himself surrounded by unknown horsemen sneaking up on his camp in the dead of night.

It was to his credit that he didn't give himself away with a shout and a run for the shadows away from the fire.

And even more so that now he was trying to waken and warn his partner.

Longarm was positive that was what he was doing.

That faked nudge on the other man's shoulder was enough to get the second man to moving too now.

Longarm guessed there was some frightened whispering going on in that camp right about now.

Sheriff Walker, though, riding a few yards to Longarm's left, seemed unaware that the two men in the camp were now alert.

Longarm had resolved not to interfere in this posse business in any way, shape, or form.

All he wanted was to get this thing seen through and then get on the first available train to Denver. Or possibly the second, depending on Mrs. Hosmer's inclinations.

Now . . . well, if the posse went bolting in on top of those fellows out of the night without any kind of announcement, there could be needless hell to pay.

Those boys on the ground could have guns under their soogans with them. Probably did. And if they didn't know it was the law that had come calling, there could be some mighty justifiable self-defense going on. On *both* sides of the fight.

Longarm glanced over toward Walker, but the big man seemed disinclined to announce their presence openly. Apparently he wanted to "capture" these boys while they were still groggy with sleep. The man seemed not to realize that it was already much too late for that. He still believed them to be unaware of the posse.

Longarm chewed on his moustache for a moment. He still didn't want to get involved with this posse business. Sure as hell didn't want to muddy the waters with announcements of authority or a takeover of the posse effort.

But he didn't want anybody shot either.

With a tight smile, Longarm shifted all his weight to one side, dropped his boot out of the stirrup, and soundly kicked his own horse in the foreleg.

The animal reacted by first stumbling and then jumping sideways with a snort of alarm and a flurry of churning hooves.

"Oh, hell!" Longarm said loudly. And then, quickly, "I'm sorry, Sheriff. Sheriff Walker? I'm sorry 'bout that, Sheriff."

He said it loud enough to be heard a hundred yards away.

Walker gave him a glare that could have withered a garlic clove.

"Don't anybody shoot, boys," Longarm said just as loudly. "It's just me and the sheriff over here."

Longarm could hear some confused hoofbeats on the far side of the fire, but it was the two figures under the soogans he was watching closely. They stirred again briefly, then lay very still. He suspected—hoped—there was some more whispered discussion going on over by that campfire.

Walker gave in to the inevitable now that the sneak was blown. The sheriff stood tall in his stirrups and announced himself in a loud, commanding tone.

Immediately the two men by the fire sat upright, letting

their soogans fall to their waists and revealing the dark gleam of oiled metal lying—on the ground, thank goodness—beside the saddles they were using for pillows.

"Come ahead," one of them called.

"Move in, boys, and cover them," Walker called out. "You by the fire. Move away from them guns. I can see 'em, y'know. Move away from 'em now, slow and easy. No sense you getting shot before your trial. No need in that at all."

The two men by the fire looked confused. They were closer to being boys than men, Longarm could see now. They neither reached for their revolvers nor moved anywhere else. They just sat there, confused and no doubt partially blinded by the firelight so close to them, while the possemen closed the ring around them until the two boys were staring up wide-eyed and blinking at the immensely tall figures of eight horsemen standing over them. Seven of those men, Ron Deal among them, had revolvers drawn and leveled down at the youngsters. It would be a hell of a thing to wake up to, Longarm thought.

"What . . .?"

"Shut up," Walker snapped. "I'll ask the questions. Somebody get their guns."

Quickly the two young men who had volunteered for the posse volunteered to perform this chore too. They dismounted and pulled the two boys upright, away from their beds. There were holstered revolvers by each saddle, but no other weapons.

The two prisoners were left standing barefoot and hatless, wearing only their jeans and undershirts to sleep in. Longarm did not think the evening air particularly chill, but both of them began to shiver.

Someone else dismounted and built the fire up with chunks of dried cow patties that the boys had left piled ready for a morning fire. The dried manure gave off a thin, pale light from its low flame.

"Where's the rest of the gang?" Walker demanded.

The boys only looked at each other blankly.

Walker dismounted and tossed his reins to Longarm,

who had also stepped down to the ground now.

At closer range and with more light from the fire, Long-arm could see that neither of these youngsters likely had seen his twentieth birthday. They were tousle-haired and frightened, shifting from one bootless foot to the other and hugging themselves with their arms in futile attempts to stop their shivering.

Both had pale hair, one blond and the other with a strawberry-colored mop, and they looked alike enough to be brothers, both of them lanky built and narrow-chested. The one with the reddish hair had a sprinkling of freckles across the bridge of his nose and down both cheeks.

"Where's the rest of the gang?" Walker demanded again. He stepped forward and cuffed the nearer prisoner on the side of the head.

"Hey!" The kid raised a hand toward his ear, and Walker hit him again.

That was too much for the other prisoner. With a yelp of protest, he launched himself at the sheriff.

The possemen threw themselves into it too, and for a minute or so there was considerable grunting and biting going on.

The two boys could not take on six grown men, though, and the fray was short-lived. It ended with the two boys being held with their arms pinned behind them and Sheriff Walker in front of them giving them murderous glares.

Longarm continued to stand where he was, holding his reins and Sheriff Walker's, while Marshal Deal kept his distance but held a Colt ready in his hand. Longarm had little doubt that the marshal would shoot if either of the boys broke away.

"Don't you think...," Longarm began when there seemed to be some order to the scene again, but Deal cut him off with a snapped, "Shut up."

That surprised Longarm. He figured Deal to be the savvy one of this bunch.

Walker was ignoring him anyway. The sheriff paced up and down before the boys for a minute or so. Then he spun and stuck a pointed finger under the nose of the blond boy.

"I asked you a question, damn you. Where's the rest of your bunch?"

"There ain't no rest of our bunch, mister. 'Less you mean the boys we come north with. We all paid off in Belle Fourche, an' we got no idea what happened to the rest of the crew. Me and Dolan here are headed to—"

He did not have time to finish. Walker backhanded him across the mouth to shut him up.

Behind Walker, Longarm began to fidget. This was not going well. He looked over toward Deal, who certainly should have more sense than to allow this, but the Washington marshal showed no expression at all on his lean face.

"Search their things," Walker snapped.

The boys' soogans were quickly thrown open, their saddlebags unstrapped, and the contents dumped onto the thick layers of quilted cloth.

If anyone seriously expected to find the bank's money there, they were disappointed.

The saddlebags contained a little food, a small sack of gumdrops and another of horehound candy, a handful of cartridges, one spare horseshoe and some nails, one pair of socks that needed darning, and, between them, just over a hundred dollars in coin.

"Leave that be!" one of the boys protested when Kurt gathered up the money and held it out for the sheriff to inspect.

"Shut up," Walker said. The sheriff squinted and peered closely at the money, as if there might be some difference between one coin and the next.

"Gave you a helluva small cut, didn't they?"

"Cut? Cut of what, damn you? That's what we got left outa our pay. Timmy and me rode three months with the Carson and Jaynes outfit bringing a bunch of mixed stockers up to the Musselshell. That's what we got left outa our pay, and—"

"Don't you lie t' me, boy," the sheriff snarled.

"But I'm not . . ."

The posseman who was holding him from behind stifled

the protest by yanking on the boy's pinioned arms until he yelled in pain.

"You are gonna tell me where t' find the rest of your gang, boys, or by God I'll turn the both of you over to these good folks and let 'em do what they want with you. An' believe me, that wouldn't be pretty. Not after what you done back in town."

Longarm felt a chill sweep through his belly at the response that one drew from the posse members. There was a growl of raw hate from them.

And someone earlier had said something about hanging.

"Town!" the redhaired Timmy wailed. "Mister, we ain't seen a town in better'n a week. Longer. We don't know—" The man who was holding him jerked on his arms again. Timmy paled and would have fallen to his knees if the posseman had not been holding him upright.

This time, though, the kid was prepared for it. He clamped his jaw hard shut and refused to cry out from the pain, although it was enough to bring tears to his eyes. He was doing his best to keep any of the posse members from seeing it.

"I've asked you nice," Walker said in a low voice, "and I've warned you fair. We know damn good and well you two was part of that holdup gang. We got the proof of it right here in our hands with part of the loot you stole. Now, damn it, you got the choice to make. You tell me what I want t' know." He paused menacingly. "Or I turn my back on this affair an' let these poor boys who you've wiped out an' whose friends you've shot down like dogs in the street, either you tell me what I got to know or I turn you over to 'em."

Longarm looked toward Deal.

The marshal had more sense than this fat, elected asshole.

Surely Deal would stop Harlan Walker.

Marshal Ron Deal uncocked his Colt and put it away, then reached into his pocket for a cheroot. He looked at Longarm. "Got a light?" The man acted like he was completely uninterested in what was happening here.

71

Longarm felt his gut tighten. It was easy to image what those poor boys must be feeling. Because no matter what Harlan Walker and his posse believed, it was dead certain that these two cowboys couldn't, just could *not* be part of the gang that had robbed the bank and the train back in Washington. Not and be out here alone, showing a fire in the night and having only a hundred dollars between them as their split of the successful robberies.

Could Harlan Walker be so damned anxious for an arrest and a reputation for success that he would deliberately let two innocent youngsters die to bolster his own chances of reelection?

No, damn it. Longarm couldn't believe that of Walker or any other lawman.

But he *could* believe that the poor fool was stupid enough to believe this crap he was spouting.

"Make up your minds," Walker ordered.

One of the eager volunteers in the posse pulled a hemp catch rope off the nearest saddle and began trying to fashion a hangman's noose with it.

Worst of all, this posse was not loud and bullying.

They were not wasting time with shouts and threats and blustering.

They were actually going to do it.

Marshal Deal turned his back and walked off into the shadows. A moment later Longarm could hear a thin stream of fluid splashing on the ground. When he was done Deal remained where he was, and Sheriff Walker went off to join him.

It was perfectly obvious what they were doing.

The two so-called peace officers were literally turning their backs on the situation by the fire. What they did not see they could pretend not to know about.

The volunteer who had been trying to make a hangman's noose gave up on the attempt, slipped the free end of the rope through its hondo, and dropped the loop over the head of the blond boy named Dolan.

"Jesus," one of the cowboys whispered.

Chapter 10

This couldn't go on. Just couldn't.

Even if he no longer considered himself a peace officer,
Longarm damn sure still considered himself a man.

There was no way he could stand by and allow a bunch
of ignorant yahoos like these hang two men by mistake.

He looked toward where Deal and Walker had been, but
the two local law officers had walked off into the darkness
somewhere.

Longarm palmed his Colt and stepped forward.

"Whoa," he said in a low voice. "You boys don't know
what you're doing, and if you keep on you'll make the
kind of mistake that you can't apologize for later."

"What the hell—"

"You heard what these kids said. They're a couple of
cowboys between jobs. Surely you can see—"

"We heard what Sheriff Walker said, too, mister. Now

you put that thing away," one of the possemen said.

"Look at 'im, Bill," another of the posse members, one of the reluctant appointees, put in. "Why, I'll bet he's part of the gang. Prob'ly was in town scouting the whole deal for them. That's what I'll bet."

Longarm shook his head in pure disbelief. "You boys just get ignoranter and ignoranter, don't you? First you think these kids with their few dollars are part of the gang. Now you think I am. If you'd all settle down, we could take these fellows to town so the victims could get a look at them and their horses. That should prove whether they were part of the gang or not. And when it was all over, you could give their stuff back and let them go on their way. Now, what could be the objection to that?"

"I'll tell you what, damn you. You're just hoping we'll get so busy with you and these thieves here that we'll let the rest of the crowd get away. Why, I'll bet you're all s'posed to meet someplace to divvy up the money you stole from us. Of course that's what it is."

Longarm still wanted to reason with them, to get them to do something sensible here. Now that Sheriff Walker had put them on the scent, though, all they could smell was blood.

"You son of a bitch," one of them said. "We'll hang them an' you too. Then we'll catch up with the rest of your murderin' gang."

The man looked like he was ready to haul his gun out, but Longarm slowed him down with a close look at the business end of a .44 Colt.

"All you have to do," Longarm said patiently, "is take them back for a fair hearing in front of witnesses and a judge. That's all. If it turns out I'm wrong, there's no harm done. They'll still be in legal custody. But if you hang them now, and it turns out later that you're wrong . . . boys, there's no coming back from a mistake like that. You can't resurrect a dead man and tell him you're sorry, you made a little mistake. You aren't going to play that game here. I won't let you do it."

"We know what you're up to, mister. You're trying to

keep us from doing our bounden duty. You're trying to let these ones and the rest of the gang escape."

"I keep trying to tell you, boys—"

Longarm was interrupted by the sound of a gunshot from off in the direction Walker and Deal had gone.

One of them must have noticed what was happening and thrown a shot, although whether at Longarm or at the two cowboys he was not sure.

Wherever the shot had been aimed, it went into the fire, throwing sparks and bits of burning manure into the air and scattering the whole damned posse in all directions as the slug came close to everybody in the group.

Longarm was not of a mind to shoot it out with two lawmen, no matter their ignorance, but neither was he interested in standing idly around while one of them shot him or the cowboys.

When the possemen jumped, so did Longarm. He snatched the hemp loop off the nearer boy's neck and shoved both of them away from the ring of firelight.

"Grab the nearest pony, and let's get the hell out of here," he barked.

The boys might have been confused by all that had happened to them since they woke, but they were in no hurry to die. Once they had the chance, they jumped.

Another shot came out of the darkness, and now one of the possemen fired from much closer range.

Whoever was shooting from the distance apparently was trying to avoid hitting one of his own men, though, and the posseman close up was just plain a poor shot. Neither bullet connected.

Longarm slowed them all down by throwing several shots into the night, aiming deliberately high so no one would be injured.

Right now all he wanted was time enough to let this business settle so it could be handled properly by a court of law and a judge who was not excited by the stupidities of the moment.

"Come on, boys. Stick with me."

Longarm grabbed for the reins of Ron Deal's horse,

75

which was far and away the best of the lot, while the two cowboys took hold of whatever they could reach. Their own saddles were still lying at the heads of their soogans, and their horses were who-knew-where, on hobbles or a picket rope.

"Come on," Longarm urged as he leaped into Deal's saddle without take time to find the stirrup.

Beside him both cowboys were scrambling onto horses as well, abandoning everything except the jeans and drawers they were wearing. It was plain damn lucky that no one had thought to tie their hands yet, but that oversight allowed the getaway.

Longarm wheeled his horse—his stolen horse, if it came right down to it, but he could straighten that out some other time; right now it was the least of his worries —and threw another couple discouraging shots toward the rising moon.

"This way." He leaned low over the neck of Ron Deal's roan and booted the animal into a belly-down run, directing the horse straight into the bunch of loose horses standing nearby and scattering them by emptying his Colt into the air. That would help slow the pursuit while Walker and Deal and company chased loose horses in the dark.

Behind Longarm, the cowboys raced close at his heels, as if his dark figure was their only hope of salvation. As in fact, at that moment, it probably was.

Longarm rode hard for a mile, then sat upright on Ron Deal's saddle and slowed the roan to a lope. What with the confusion of the scattered horses behind them and the cover of darkness, he figured that should be safe enough, and he did not want to overtire the horses.

The two cowboys were still sticking close behind him.

He motioned them to his side. "Just because I happen to believe you're innocent, it doesn't necessarily follow that you are," he told them. "So I want you to consider yourselves in my custody till we get this worked out."

"It beats hanging, mister," one of them said.

"Yeah, I expect it does."

They breasted a rise and dropped down to the bottom to

splash through a small creek.

"Stop here for a minute," Longarm said.

Obediently, both cowboys brought their horses to a halt and let the animals drink.

Longarm dismounted and knelt to take a drink himself while Deal's horse had its fill.

"I can't know," he said, "but it could be that business back there wouldn't have happened if anybody'd carried water along today. Those boys'd been drinking some, but not water. That might've affected their judgment."

He said it, but he was not so sure he fully believed it. No one had had *that* much to drink.

Marshal Deal, in particular, had been sober enough. Yet he had gone along with Sheriff Walker's bullying and the possemen's cold anger. That still surprised Longarm. He had expected better from Deal after the man's earlier displays of good sense.

Still, there was no help for it now but to try to keep himself and these two boys alive until he could get to some real law and get this situation off his hands.

Longarm remounted and turned south, back toward the railroad.

What he needed was a town. Civilization. Courts and real law.

The only big problem with that was that he had damn little idea of where he was, much less where the nearest town other than Washington would be.

As far as he could recall, he had never heard of Washington, Nebraska before. And considering the way he had left the U.P. train the other evening, he still didn't know where it was in relation to anything else along the rails.

Still, there had to be other towns in the vicinity of the tracks. And the railroad lay to the south.

"We've got some riding to do so we can get out of this mess," Longarm said. "While we're doing it, I'd like to hear some explanations from you fellas. Who are you and why should I think you *aren't* part of the gang that pulled those robberies?"

The boys were riding close on either side of Longarm,

77

seemingly grateful for both his help and his company now.

"I'm Sam Dolan," the redhaired one said. "My pard here is Timmy Ryan. Like we tried to tell those other fellas, we come up with a trail drive out of south Texas working for Mr. Terrell Hawkins, he was the trail boss, of Carson and Jaynes in Frio, Texas. We paid off at Belle Fourche, split up there after delivering the herd up on the Musselshell and carryin' the remuda back that far to sell them, and we was on our way home. Just kinda, you know, riding along and seeing some country."

"Is there any way you could prove that?"

"Sure. Course Mr. Hawkins won't be home yet, but I reckon a feller could wire down to the Carson and Jaynes headquarters. We're on their books from when the herd left the Three Rivers country."

Longarm grunted. It was something that could be verified easily enough. Not that he doubted these boys. Harlan Walker's suspicions were foolish in the extreme. But once Walker laid the charge it would take facts to disprove the sheriff's accusations no matter what the law said about innocence until guilt was proven.

Hard reality said that in cases like this it was the innocence that had to be proved.

"That herd left a long time ago," Longarm observed, playing the devil's advocate. "I don't suppose you can prove where you were this morning, can you?"

"No, sir," Ryan admitted. "We been riding together this whole day, but I don't recollect that we seen anybody the whole day long except each other."

"No cowboys? No farmers?" Longarm asked.

"No, sir. Nothing except some cows and some pronghorns."

"And one badger," Dolan added.

"Yes, sir. And that one badger."

Longarm sighed. That didn't help matters. Still, any fair and sensible man should be able to see that there wasn't anything that could be held against these boys except lousy luck at being in the way of Walker's posse.

"Well, what we've got to do now is get you to a town

where you can have the protection of the law until these charges against you are dropped."

"Charges, sir? But we ain't done nothing to be charged with."

Longarm smiled at him. "Now you have. So've I, for that matter. Escaping from the custody of the law is a crime itself, and I would have to say that you damn sure done that."

"Oh." Ryan sounded worried.

Longarm laughed. "As it happens, though . . . and those gentlemen who by now oughta be chasing us somewhere back there don't know it . . . as it happens, I have a way around that one. You're *still* in the custody of the law."

"We are?"

Longarm introduced himself. And this time he did not hold back the title that was still his to use until he submitted that resignation.

"I sure am glad you was along with that crowd, Marshal," Dolan said with feeling.

"Maybe it didn't turn out so bad after all," Longarm admitted.

They continued to move south at a swift, easy lope.

With Sheriff Harlan Walker in charge of the posse behind them, Longarm did not think they had to worry a lick about anyone catching them before they could reach the safety of a town other than Washington.

Chapter 11

Breakfast was the last of the hardtack Longarm had been given, shared among the three of them, and some gritty water sieved from a hole the boys dug in the soft sand at the bottom of the draw they were following. They continued to travel the course of the creek they had discovered the night before, but the surface water had disappeared underground somewhere in the miles to the rear.

"I've had better to start my day," Sam Dolan observed quietly. He was not exactly an imposing figure of prosperity as he sat hunkered next to a thicket of wild plum near the makeshift water hole. He looked like an Arkansas farm boy with his light hair falling over his forehead and his bare feet. Everything the boys owned from boots to hats and all that had been in between had been abandoned to the posse.

"Had worse too," Timmy Ryan put in.

Dolan grinned at him. "So we have."

"Well, this should be over and done with soon enough," Longarm told them. He was chewing slowly on the last biscuit of hardtack, trying to make it last and pretend he had been well and properly fed for the past several days. But then he too had experienced hard times in the past. Once more was not going to cause permanent harm, and a little temporary discomfort was not worth bitching about. "Soon as we get to the rails we're as good as safe. We just turn east to the nearest town, and I have a few words with the local law there."

"What about our things, Marshal? We worked awful hard for that money. Not to say nuthin' about our saddles an' horses an' things." The freckle-faced Ryan seemed more concerned about the future now than about the present predicament.

"I can't make you any promises that aren't mine to keep," Longarm answered honestly, "but I can't see how any fair-minded court wouldn't return them to you."

"Courts ain't always fair-minded," Dolan put in.

"Maybe," Longarm admitted, "but what we got sure beats anything else I've ever heard tell of."

"I reckon," Dolan said dourly.

Longarm stood, his knee joints creaking. He counted the slim cheroots remaining in his pocket—there were half a dozen—and decided they should reach civilization soon enough that he could afford to smoke one now. When he had it alight he said, "Soon as the horses are done watering we can get along."

The horses were fresh after the few hours of rest Longarm had permitted them. They were already saddled. Longarm had taken the precaution of leaving them saddled although with loose cinches on the off chance that Harlan Walker and crowd might blunder their way onto the cold camp Longarm and the boys had established in the pre-dawn hours.

"Snug them down now, and let's go. I want to get shut of this and on to more interesting things." Whatever those things might be, Longarm added silently to himself.

"Yes, sir." The young cowboys pulled their rimfire cinches snug and swung onto their saddles with the fluid ease of born horsemen.

Longarm led the way south. He was already in the saddle before it occurred to him that perhaps they should fill in the water hole they had sunk in the dry creekbed. No point in it, though, he decided. That posse should be miles in the wrong direction by now, the sheriff's tracking abilities being what they were, and perhaps some cow or whitetail would have need of that water before the sand sides of the hole caved in or got covered over by the next flash flow of rainwater runoff.

He yawned as he rode. They had sure missed some sleep lately.

But that was no more of a problem than the shortage of groceries. One good meal and one good flop, and both those discomforts would be so far behind that it would be difficult to remember them clearly.

"Oh, hell," Longarm muttered. "Back! *Back this way.*" He spun Ron Deal's roan back over its hocks and rammed the steel to the animal.

Sam Dolan, riding close behind him, hesitated with his eyes wide and his jaw sagging open in unasked question. Ryan, a little further back, reacted more quickly, spinning his horse back the way they had just come and thumping the animal with his bare heels.

There was a sharp sound on the air like grease sizzling in a hot pan except louder and quicker, and immediately afterward a spurt of dust flew from the ground between Longarm's horse and Ryan's as the lead slug tore into the soft earth.

"Shit," Dolan blurted. He needed no extra urging now to snatch his horse around in a run for safety.

The bullet had struck the ground and Dolan had time enough to react to it before they heard the sound of the gunshot.

The shooter had fired from much too great a distance. Not that Longarm was complaining about the man's impatience.

Longarm had not really thought there was danger ahead. He had spotted a reflection from the top of that rise, a glint of the early sunlight on glass or metal, and only his habitual caution made him decide to change their course and ride wide around the reflection. But in truth he had thought it most likely that the light had picked out a fleck of mica or a discarded whiskey bottle.

Instead there was someone back there shooting at them.

Another bullet cut the grass in front of them. The range was too long for accurate shooting, but whoever was back there did not mind wasting some powder to chance.

"Zig-zag," Longarm shouted. "Weave back and forth. Make it harder for him to draw a lead on you."

A slug droned past Longarm close enough for him to hear. He did not see where it struck. He took his own advice and turned the roan toward the right a bit, then after a dozen strides swung it left again.

Ahead of him the cowboys were doing the same now.

They dashed over a wrinkle in the surface of the ground and dropped out of sight of the distant rifleman, continued their run back down to the protection of some crackwillow clinging to life in the dry streambed they had followed through the night, and finally drew rein there.

"Oh, Jesus," Timmy Ryan moaned. He was pale and shaken.

"Are you hit, boy?"

Ryan bit his underlip and squeezed his eyes shut, but he shook his head. "No-n-no, sir. I don't think so."

"Dolan?"

"No. Just damn lucky, though. We could've all been—"

"We could've all been born rich too, but we weren't," Longarm snapped.

He stood in his stirrups to peer toward the sheltering rise that separated them from the gunman's position. But there was nothing to see back there except grass and sky and one small, puffy cloud floating in the air off to the southwest.

84

"Come on." He led off at a lope, this time moving to the east and a shade north again.

And this time keeping a very close eye on everything around them.

The question was, he kept thinking over and over again, *how the hell had anybody gotten in front of them like that?*

And would they be as lucky if it happened a second time?

"I don' know about you, but I'm getting pretty damn hungry," Sam Dolan complained.

"Hush." Longarm was trying to concentrate, and Dolan's bitching did not help a hell of a lot.

Timmy Ryan was not so much of a complainer. He just stood there with a stricken, pitiful look about him, as if he was ready to turn into a jelly of trembles at any moment now.

"Do you see them?" Ryan asked nervously.

"No," Longarm answered curtly.

"Sorry."

Longarm supposed he should have felt some sympathy for the kid, tried to reassure him, but right now he hadn't time for all that.

Right now he was busy enough just trying to make sure the three of them survived.

He stood now, his Stetson held in one hand so there was less to show above the skyline, on the back slope of the rise they had just crossed. Only his eyes and the top of his head would have been visible from the other side of that rise.

From where they now were he had a clear line of sight for three quarters of a mile or a little better. If the posse was still in pursuit of them, he would be able to see the riders coming at least that far away. That was plenty enough gap between hunter and pursued given the way Walker used his horses. In the meantime Longarm's— well, Ron Deal's—horse and those being ridden by Ryan and Dolan were gaining rest.

Longarm had expected the posse to be only minutes behind them after the attempted ambush off to the southwest of where they now were, but after twenty minutes or more there still was no sign of pursuit.

It was disquieting, Longarm found.

Sheriff Harlan Walker had surprised him once.

He really did not want it to happen a second time.

"Can I ask you something, Marshal?" Dolan inquired.

Longarm sighed, then gave in. It didn't look like the posse was chasing them anyway. "Yeah."

"I was thinkin', like, if something was to happen to you or, well, you know what I mean. Me and Timmy would be hung out to dry. Legally speakin', that is. So what I was wondering, Marshal, was if you could kinda deputize us or whatever it is you do, and maybe mark out a paper to that effect, so if we got caught by those buzzards and you wasn't around to speak for us . . ."

If Longarm was dead was what he meant, but he did not want to put it into words.

"I can't do that, Sam," Longarm said, still keeping his vigil along their back trail. "In the first place, I haven't any authority to do it. Remember, technically speaking here, you boys are suspected criminals, charged by a duly constituted local authority with the commission of serious crimes. Now, mind, I happen to believe you, but until a judge says *he* believes you, what I think won't carry a spoonful of water.

"Secondly, even if you weren't accused of any crime, we aren't chasing anybody. *We're* the ones doing the running. I could only deputize somebody else in an emergency and then only to help me make an arrest. Sheriff Walker and his men aren't the ones as have committed any crimes. They been stupid as hell, I know, but they haven't done anything illegal." Longarm softened his refusal with a smile. "Good thing, too, that the law doesn't hold stupidity against a man. We'd all of us be behind bars at least part of the time. Some of us *most* of the time."

Dolan frowned. "If you couldn't do that, maybe we could at least borry that Winchester of yours. Give us something to defend ourselves with if it came to it."

Tim Ryan became even paler at that suggestion, but he said nothing.

Again Longarm shook his head.

"But—" Dolan tried to protest.

"I won't argue it with you, Sam. Two reasons again. Firstly, like I've already explained I thought nice and clear, you boys are prisoners in my custody. And you'd best remember that little point and hold onto it, because that's the only thing that makes what I'm trying to do for you halfway legal. Second thing is, we aren't going to shoot back at that posse."

"But . . ."

"I know. You don't have to remind me. They shot at us first. Do we give them a chance, they'll shoot at us again. That doesn't matter. We don't shoot back. Cut and dried. No matter what they do, boys, we can't shoot back at them."

"That's a helluva attitude," Dolan grumbled.

"Maybe so, Sam, but that's the way it is. Wrongheaded and dumb as I think they are, they're still the law and they are doing what they feel is right. They don't know any different. I do. I won't be shooting any of them."

"Even if they kill me or Timmy? Even if they kill the both of us?"

"Even so. I won't shoot at any of them."

"Well, shit!" Dolan reached up to snatch his hat off and throw it down on the ground, remembered too late that he had no hat to show his temper with, and had to settle for stomping his feet instead.

Even that was something of a mistake. With no boots on feet unaccustomed to being without the protection of a cobbler's handiwork, Dolan stamped hard on something more solid than grass and loose sand, gave out a short yip of pain, and began to hobble in circles.

Longarm turned his head away to keep the boys from seeing the smile that he could not suppress.

"We'll give it ten minutes more," he said as if nothing had happened. "If they don't show by then we'll swing east a ways and try for the railroad again."

"Yes, sir," Timmy Dolan said unhappily.

"I don't suppose either of you fellows has any notion where we can find water or something to eat in this country?"

"Noplace closer than the camp we run from last night," Ryan said.

"Then while we ride, I'll do the watching for the posse. You concentrate on trying to find something edible."

"Such as?"

"Hell, any damn thing. A bird nest with unhatched eggs. A prairie dog town where we might dig something out of the holes. Whatever. I have the Winchester but I'd rather not be making loud noises if we can avoid it. No telling who could hear and maybe get us in trouble."

Both boys sighed. They did not look happy.

That was all right. Longarm was not feeling a hell of a lot of happy himself right now.

"If you like, you can go on down and scout around the slope to see if you can find anything. I want to keep watch for a little longer. Then I'll come down and join you."

"And if we try and take off on you?" Dolan challenged.

"Then you'll have *two* law parties after you," Longarm said softly. "And I don't think you'd find me as easy to get shut of as Harlan Walker."

"C'mon, Sam," Timmy Ryan urged, tugging at his friend's elbow.

"Sometimes," Timmy said as the boys led their horses down the hill and probably thought themselves out of Longarm's hearing, "sometimes I wisht you'd learn t' keep your jaw shut, Sam."

Longarm could not hear Dolan's answer, but he could make a pretty fair guess at what it would have been.

He used the back of his hand to wipe some sweat out of his eyes—he was not used to being bareheaded in the sun any more than the cowboys were—and resumed his watch along their back trail.

So far there was nothing back there to see.

And in a way, that was more worrisome than an out-and-out horse race would have been.

88

When a man doesn't know where his enemy is, he just naturally has to figure that the son of a bitch is up to something.

The question now was: what?

Chapter 12

Lunch was a drink of silt-laden water, gritty with sand and who knew what else, and a tightening of Longarm's belt buckle. At least he had a belt to tighten. Timmy Ryan had removed his before going to sleep and had had to abandon it when the posse appeared.

This time Longarm covered over the small hole they had dug to reach the water that seeped beneath the dry, sandy surface of this nearly barren country.

Sam Dolan sat on the ground nearby while Longarm erased the more obvious signs that they had stopped at the spot. "I don't know why you're botherin' to do that, Marshal. Don't look to me like anybody's behind us now. I think we give them the slip."

"Do you happen to know where that posse is right now or what they're up to?" Longarm asked him.

"Nope. No better'n you do."

"My point exactly. We don't know, and until or unless we do, then 'don't look' and 'think' don't cut no ice worth a damn. What we'd better do is assume they're coming along after us and try to make it just a little bit harder for them. This isn't easy country to track through. No point in us making them a present of it until we know we're safe."

Dolan grumbled some and made no offer to help. His partner, though, pitched in and made sure the manure piles left by their standing horses were scattered so that they would not be so obviously fresh to anyone passing by.

"That's right, Ryan. You're getting the idea," Longarm said as the youngster kicked the horseapples to scatter them. "Mount up now."

They rode eastward after their moist but unsatisfying lunch until midafternoon, when Longarm turned south again toward the rails somewhere in the distance. His lack of knowledge of their whereabouts was a handicap here, and the boys from Texas were no help at all. They had gone north on the Ogallala Trail far to the west and had been drifting home without any particular plan or pattern, just moving south and east in the general direction of Texas. They had no more idea than Longarm did about where they were in relation to the towns of Nebraska.

Late in the day Longarm stopped them and eased his own horse up a slight rise so he could get a look at the country ahead of them.

"Something's out there, but I can't make out what it is," he said in a low voice as the boys followed in spite of his instructions. They seemed to want to stick close to him in case of trouble.

"I see it too," Ryan said. "Somethin' flickering now and again. Could be sunlight catching the fan blades on a windmill."

"Shit, man, let's go, then. If there's a ranch we can get something t' eat," Dolan put in. He sounded eager about something for the first time that day.

Longarm grunted. Ryan could be right. That now-and-then flickering could well be the slanting rays of sunshine

92

from the late afternoon catching the blades of a moving windmill.

Or it could be something else.

"We'll ease on up there," he decided, "but we'll do it slow, and we'll keep out of sight from whatever it is."

"I sure hope they've butchered recent," Dolan said. "If they haven't, I'd be pleased t' do the chore for them." He swallowed hard, and Longarm knew exactly what he was experiencing. The mere thought of fresh beef fried in its own tallow was enough to get Longarm's mouth to watering. He began to salivate heavily, the swallowed spit lying uncomfortable in his empty belly until it threatened to give him stomach cramps.

"Stay behind me," Longarm warned, "and don't show yourselves unless I say so."

"Yes, sir," Ryan answered.

Dolan said nothing.

They rode south again, Longarm in the lead and picking their way with care, staying with the lowest ground possible to avoid being seen by anyone who might have been posted to watch for them.

Longarm could not help remembering that Walker's suddenly sensible posse had gotten ahead of them once before. This too could be a trap.

Those "windmill" blade flashes could as easily be stray reflections from some kind of heliotrope signal.

The suspicion might have been a case of stretching caution to an extreme, but better that than to take foolish chances that could cost lives.

All they needed to get out of this mess was a bit of civilization and a fair hearing on the subject. But first they had to reach it.

In the meantime, Longarm did not intend to risk his own life or the lives of the Texas cowboys. Not a lick more than he had to with a proddy posse chasing them and ready to shoot without warning. That much had been demonstrated already. And Longarm could not shoot back if it happened again.

When he thought they had come far enough, Longarm removed his Stetson and held it down by his thigh while he eased the horse forward until he could see across the rolling grass to where the movement had been.

Relief flowed through him when he saw that Ryan had been right.

It was a moving windmill they had seen. The breeze was coming from behind them, carrying sound with it, or they probably would already have heard the creaking and groaning of the slowly spinning fan.

He moved a few feet higher on the slope until he could see the entire tower and the country beyond it.

A group of spotted cattle, longhorns mixed with some other, beefier breed, were gathered at the base of the windmill around a water tank.

Of much greater interest, though, there was the low roof of a sod house visible now a half mile or so beyond the windmill and tank.

It was coming evening now and would be dark soon. As Longarm watched there was a thin billow of pale smoke from a chimney set in the roof of the soddy. Someone was in there preparing supper.

Again Longarm could feel the saliva begin to flow in his mouth. His belly ached with hunger.

"Come on," Longarm said softly. "But stick behind me. Whoever lives down there may've been told to look out for us. If so they'll think we're thieves and murderers and who knows what else. They'd shoot on sight. So you boys lay back and let me handle it."

"Not very damn likely," Dolan grumbled. "Hell, we ain't done anything."

"I believe that, but I don't remember it slowing that posse any. You just do what I say."

"You're actin' like an old woman," Dolan said.

"Maybe. But I've known some old women that were pretty smart. *Live* old women."

"Bullshit."

They rode in silence until they broke into full view of

the little hardscrabble homestead, about a quarter-mile out from it.

It was nearly dark by then, but they could make out the soddy cut into the side of the low hill, the wall of a hand-dug well in the yard near the house, and a small corral with a shed or shelter of some sort built next to it.

Yellow lamplight spilled out of the open doorway of the soddy, and a dimly seen figure was moving between the well and the house.

"Hot damn," Dolan yelped. He stood in his stirrups and leaned forward.

"No—" Longarm leaned to the side and tried to snatch the reins of Dolan's horse as the youngster kicked his animal forward, but Dolan passed him just inches too far away.

"Come back here, damn you!"

"Ain't nobody laying for us up there, and there's supper on the table," Dolan threw back at him happily.

Ryan acted like he was going to race ahead with his partner, then gave Longarm a worried look and thought better of it. He checked his horse, which had tried to spurt ahead with the other animal.

They were within a couple hundred yards of the soddy now.

The person who had been walking from the well must have been alerted by the sound of Dolan's yip or by the noise of the cowboy's horse.

The figure dropped something to the ground, probably a water bucket, and sprinted for the protection of the house. It was too dark by now to make out if it was a man or a woman.

"Damn you, Dolan," Longarm barked uselessly toward Dolan's back. Even if the posse had not passed the word for people to be on the lookout for a trio of murderers, anyone charging a house out of the night would raise suspicions with the occupants.

"Well, shit," Longarm grumped. He kicked his horse into a lope. It was already too late to make a quiet, peaceful approach, as he had intended. Dolan had ruined that.

Longarm had wanted to approach the place alone, with his hat in one hand and his badge in the other, so he could have a word with the rancher. Just in case.

But now Dolan was thundering into the ranch yard, leaving the saddle even before his horse was brought to a full halt, and running for the lighted doorway of the soddy.

Maybe . . .

The light coming through the doorway suddenly intensified and expanded, gushing out fan-shaped and very bright as a weapon, probably a shotgun, was fired from just inside the soddy.

The slug or shot charge took Sam Dolan full in the chest as he ran toward the house.

There was just enough light remaining in the sky for Longarm and Ryan to see Dolan crumple to the ground a dozen paces short of the door.

"Oh, Jesus!" Ryan whispered. He booted his horse forward, intending to race toward his partner to help him.

"No," Longarm snapped.

This time he was able to grab Ryan's reins before the boy got by him.

"No," he repeated.

"But . . . that man's murdered Sam. Killed him in cold blood."

"No," Longarm said again. There was sadness in his voice. "No, son, what happened there was that that man defended himself. Far as he knew, Timmy, he protected his family from a murderer. He protected himself from you and Sam and me. He didn't do wrong."

"But . . ."

"Come on, son. We got to get away from here. The law will be told quick as that rancher can get the word out, and there will be a posse onto us again."

There was no sign of movement around the soddy now. The light from the doorway reached Sam Dolan's awkwardly sprawled legs, but no further. And Dolan was not moving.

The rancher was out of sight, probably terrified inside

96

the small house, holding his shotgun at the ready and determined to protect his wife or whoever might be in there with him.

Longarm thought about trying to ride close enough to the side of the place to shout explanations. To try to tell them who he was and what his business was here.

But that would not likely work.

The rancher had been frightened into killing once in self-defense this evening. There was no real likelihood he would believe an unknown voice coming at him from the night.

No, damn it, better to turn and ride away now.

There was nothing anyone could do for Sam Dolan.

Better not to make it even worse at this point.

"Come along, Timmy."

Longarm turned his horse, keeping his hold on Ryan's reins so he could lead the youngster along with him, and headed back off to the north.

Word about them was out by now, he gathered.

And once the word spread about Sam Dolan's "attack," which was surely how it would be seen, on the soddy . . . once that got out, there probably would be other posses after them from any other towns that were near.

Hell's bells, this thing could turn into a manhunt covering half of Nebraska, with Custis Long and Tim Ryan the targets of it.

"Oh, Lordy," Timmy Ryan moaned as Longarm led him out onto the dark prairie.

Chapter 13

Longarm heard Timmy Ryan crying in the night after they finally stopped for a few hours of sleep.

Sam Dolan had not been all that likeable a young man. But he had not deserved the end that came to him.

Not that that seemed to matter so much, Longarm reflected as he lay in Ron Deal's bedroll. What a man deserved very seldom had anything to do with life or with death, either one. Which was a hell of a thing if you thought about it.

Longarm cursed himself for wasting his thoughts on such unproductive matters. Better to deal with what was than to fret about the things that weren't.

The simple fact was that Sam Dolan was dead. Longarm could not see any way the boy could have taken a charge of buck square in the chest like that and not be dead.

The thing now was to keep himself and Timmy Ryan

alive until he could work out a solution to the problem Harlan Walker and his posse had put them into.

Longarm sighed. Keeping the two of them alive was not going to get any easier after that business back at the soddy.

Obviously the word had already been spread for folks to look out for the murderers from Washington.

Walker's posse was known to be in the field after them.

Now it was a fair certainty that neighboring towns would be sending out their own posses, probably better equipped and almost certainly better led than Walker's.

People in such big, nearly empty country as this worked hard at protecting themselves. Often enough they had to. And a situation like this one, when they genuinely believed that a band of gunmen was on the prowl, when they believed that one ranch had already been jumped . . . in a case like this one, the people would rally behind their local law and try to bring the murderers in.

It was just Longarm's tough luck that he was one of those being unjustly sought.

It was even tougher luck that if they were run down, he could not bring himself to shoot in his defense or Tim Ryan's.

He would not be able to do that any more than he could have ridden in on that ranch the night before and gunned down the rancher who shot Sam Dolan.

Not knowing that that rancher had been innocent and well-meaning in the affair. Wrong as hell, yes, but innocent.

It was a problem that might only get worse before it could get any better.

Making it get better—that was the thing.

That was what he had to figure out and then do.

He had to get to civilization. To authority. To a damn telegraph office if nothing else.

Billy Vail would get it straightened out quick enough. If only Longarm could reach him with word of his plight.

But that might be something of a trick.

Ordinarily Longarm could simply find a way to the telegraph wires, anywhere, at any empty spot between towns, hook up his key, and transmit to Denver.

But his damn telegraph key was tucked away in his bag, and that was back in Sara Hosmer's shop building in Washington.

Longarm lay awake staring toward some cloud that was scudding low across the sky, blocking out the bright pin-prick lights of the stars here and there.

Why the hell had Harlan Walker chosen *now* to begin acting sensible with his manhunt?

The posse was busy somewhere in this country, and they were spreading an alarm further and further with every passing hour, probably.

Twice they had been able to intercept and to thwart Longarm as he moved east from Washington and the original area of the chase. Once they were lying for him. Once their warnings cut his path.

So by now, he reasoned, they would have good reason to know that he was trying to escape toward the east.

Perhaps now the best thing would be to turn back west, even though that would mean a hell of a lot of backtrack riding without supplies or the hope of securing any.

East was where he had been hoping to find safety. Yet east was where the posse already knew him to be heading.

West would be difficult. Damned difficult considering the distances that would be involved and the hunger that already lay heavy in his belly.

Timmy Ryan was not the complainer that Dolan had been, but the kid would be hungry too. And Ryan had no shirt, no hat, not even a pair of boots.

The back-loop west would likely mean days of travel before Longarm could hope to reach someone who would listen to him without wanting to shoot first.

Still, damn it, it seemed the best among poor choices.

Particularly since he still did not know where in hell he was.

Nebraska, somewhere north of the Union Pacific right-of-way. That was all he knew for sure. It was not exactly pinpoint accuracy.

It would have to be enough.

Timmy Ryan's low sobbing subsided, and soon Longarm could hear the youngster's breathing slow and steady into the rhythms of sleep.

He closed his eyes and tried to clear his mind of the problems he would have to face tomorrow.

Tomorrow would be time enough to deal with them.

Longarm hunched his shoulders, but it was a futile gesture that did nothing to keep him warm. The cold rain had come out of nowhere, the dark clouds racing down on them from the northwest with sudden fury. The squall would be gone as quickly as it had come, but that provided no comfort now.

His coat had blocked the water only briefly. Now he was soaked to the skin. Huge, wind-driven drops of icy water drummed on the crown of his hat, spilled off the brim, and poured from it into his lap, so that even his butt was no longer dry.

How Ryan was making out with neither a shirt nor a hat was something Longarm could envision but not envy.

"Can't we hole up, Marshal?" the kid asked. He looked and sounded thoroughly miserable, and his teeth were chattering out of control.

"Point to the spot, and we'll do it."

The boy looked around, but there was nothing in any direction for him to see. Not a tree or a cutbank or a shelter of any kind to get under or even to break the force of the wind.

"Bad thing about it," Longarm said, "is that this rain will wipe the ground clean of tracks. Make it easier for anybody following."

"D'you think they're behind us?"

"Got to think that, boy, whether it's so or not."

"But d'you really think . . .?"

"Yes," Longarm said. "I do."

"Oh." The kid looked even more miserable after that, although Longarm had not thought it possible that he could.

102

"Look at the bright side," Longarm told him.

"Bright side?"

Longarm smiled. "We won't have to dig for our water for the next few days, anyhow."

"You sure know how to make a body feel better, Marshall." Ryan managed a smile in return, even though his thin shoulders were shaking from the sudden cold. If Longarm was wet, Ryan looked half drowned.

"It won't be long now. It's easing up some already."

Half an hour later they were steaming under a hot sun while the rain storm was only a line of gray mist and cloud to the east.

"Better?" Longarm asked.

"Y-y-yeah. I guess." The boy was still shaking, though, and acting like he was chilled despite the comforting warmth of the sun.

"Are you all right?"

"I'm . . . all right."

He did not sound convincing worth a damn, but there was no help for it. They had to keep going. Longarm was sure a posse would be behind them by now. If not Walker's, then another bunch from whatever town was closest to that ranch where Sam Dolan had been shot. And after the rain it would be possible for a posse to find their tracks and follow them. Unless they were lucky enough that the law was searching for them to the east still. Longarm hoped for that, but he was not optimistic enough to count on it.

Longarm removed his coat and vest, rolled them up, and tied them behind his saddle to let the sun help dry his sopping shirt.

They moved steadily on, no longer so cold, but acutely aware once again of the hunger.

Longarm's belly was knotted with cramps. Much longer without food and he would be forced to hunt, regardless of the danger of a gunshot being heard.

It did not help matters at all that they so frequently passed in sight of pronghorn antelope or an occasional bunch of wandering range cattle.

Thoughts of meat—even of the now long-gone hard-tack—haunted him.

Lunch once again, though, was only water, dipped from a surface pond that lay in a low hollow after the rain.

"See?" Longarm asked, trying to make it sound cheerful. "I told you we wouldn't have to dig for our dinner this time."

Timmy Ryan only nodded and drank again. Longarm noticed that the kid's hands were trembling. He had not really gotten over his shakes and chills after their drenching earlier in the morning, and Longarm was becoming concerned about him even though he did not complain.

Longarm's worry deepened when they remounted, and Ryan had to stab for the stirrup twice before he managed to shove his bare foot into the oxbow and boost himself into the saddle.

"You making it, boy?"

"Yes, sir. I'm making it."

Three hours later Longarm heard a dull thump and turned to see Ryan's horse standing ground-reined and motionless—and riderless—on the prairie. Timmy Ryan lay face down on the ground a few feet behind the horse. He had his arms clasped tight around himself and was shaking uncontrollably.

"Oh, shit," Longarm muttered.

He swung his horse around and stepped down to see to the boy.

Chapter 14

Hunger, exposure, perhaps some illness that he could have fought off had it not been for the cold rain storm of the morning—whatever the reason or reasons, Timmy Ryan was one damn sick kid now. He lay limp and pale under the hot sun, shivering, his teeth chattering, as if he had been caught out in the middle of winter.

What he needed, Longarm knew, was food—that most of all—and rest, warmth, and shelter, at least until he could begin a recovery.

Unconsciously Longarm glanced over his shoulder down their back trail.

Rest and warmth and shelter would be damned hard to come by with a posse on their trail. And he had to assume there were men back there hunting them. Throwing out a posse was what any sensible lawman would have done,

Longarm included, given the misunderstandings and mis-information involved here.

Longarm had to avoid them *and* take care of Timmy Ryan somehow.

He untied the bedroll that had been carried by the rider whose horse Ryan had taken that night and unfolded the bedding on the ground beside the boy's chill-wracked body.

The bedroll was a flimsy commercial affair with water-proofed canvas on one side, a woolen blanket inside, and some cotton batting sewed in between them like a quilt. Longarm used his knife to separate the blanket from the other materials, then rolled up the useless remainder and returned them to the strings behind the boy's cantle. The canvas and batting were useless, but he did not want to take the time to bury them, and he certainly did not want to leave them for the posse to find.

The blanket he folded in half and then cut at the center, slicing a large T shape in the heavy cloth so the blanket could serve as a makeshift sort of Mexican poncho.

While he worked, Longarm chided himself for not thinking of that sooner. The boy had no proper clothes to protect him from the elements. The poncho would do nicely. If Longarm had thought of this earlier, the kid might not be sick right now.

Too late to worry about that, though, he reminded him-self. And better late than not at all. The poncho could still be used as a blanket at night, or Longarm could share Ron Deal's much better made bedroll with the kid.

If, that is, they were still free and moving by night.

Longarm had nothing to offer the kid to eat, but he was able to wrap him in the poncho and use some saddle strings to belt the blanket close around him at the waist. Then he lifted him back into the saddle.

"I'm sorry to have to do this, Timmy, but we got to keep moving. It's either that or risk being shot."

"I . . . I . . . I . . ." He could not get it out between his chattering teeth and had to settle for a jerky nodding of the head. He understood. He was not complaining.

"All right. Hang onto that horn if you can, son. I'll lead your horse, so all you gotta do is set him if you can. If you feel you got to stop for a minute, make a noise. I'll go as easy as we dare."

Ryan nodded again. He was pale and his eyes were squeezed shut as he steeled himself against the fevers and chills and joint aches that filled his body.

"You're doing fine, son. Here we go now."

Longarm led on, acutely aware of the hoofprints the horses left behind now in the wake of the cleansing rain. The soft sand of the rolling prairie still took no good impression of a track, but there were no other tracks visible now on the ground behind them.

Anyone striking their trail would have no trouble following them, thanks to the damned rainfall.

"Now there's some good luck," Longarm said about an hour later. He had been trying to remember to speak to the boy often, more to encourage than to inform him. "I see some cows ahead. We'll angle over that way and see if we can lose our tracks in theirs."

The cattle, twenty-odd head of heavy-bodied crossbreds, were strung out in a long line and moving steadily toward some unseen objective.

It was coming evening, so Longarm had to assume they would be going to water, although there had been more than enough rain earlier to leave surface pools dotted frequently in the low places in any direction. There was no need for them to travel for water yet something, habit probably, was drawing them north at a steady traveling gait.

"We'll . . . no, by damn, I know what we'll try," Longarm said. He turned and smiled back at the boy but was not sure if the kid was aware enough to know it or not. He had not spoken since that one attempt when Longarm put him onto his saddle.

The kid had grit, though. He weaved and swayed weakly but clung to the saddlehorn with both hands for all he was worth and had managed to keep his balance so far.

"We'll see if we can confuse the issue here for whoever's behind us."

Still leaving those telltale hoofprints behind, Longarm slowed the pace of their travel to allow the northbound herd of cattle to cross in front of them.

As they neared the thin line of churned sand left by the passage of the cattle's hooves he deliberately veered direction slightly so that his tracks could be seen blending into theirs at an angle that would carry them toward the north in the same direction the cattle were going.

"Now what we're doing," he explained to the deathly silent boy behind him, "is trying to throw a false trail. You see, those boys running behind us will figure we know they're back there. Right?" There was no answer, but Longarm had not expected one. He continued to play at the game of cheerfully casual conversation in an attempt to make Ryan feel a bit better.

"So we let them see that we're deliberately hiding our tracks in the cattle's. No help for that, you see, because our tracks will go into those of the cattle but won't be coming out on the other side."

Ryan groaned a little, but Longarm did not think he was trying to respond.

"So they'll be able to see right off that we're trying to throw them off. And they'll see plain enough that we're showing them that we intend to swing north. Now what we *hope* they'll believe is that we're showing them the north line so we can turn back and ride south to duck them. What we hope is that they outsmart us and ride south away from the line we've let them see. But instead of that, Tim, we keep right on going the way we've deliberately let them see. Make them think we're faking north but then we really do it." Longarm laughed. "Unless they start playing double-think games. You know. Figure the same way we are an' then have to wonder will *we* think *they're* thinking so and *really* go south or . . . hell, a fella can tie himself in knots that way if he really wants. What it comes down to, we got a fifty-fifty chance to throw them off no matter which way we go. And I happen to think that these cows may be going someplace in particular for more reason than

108

just water. So what we'll do, Tim, is trail along behind them to see what they're up to."

Just about dusk the cattle came to another windmill and stock tank. Beside the tank was a pile of salt. It was the salt, not the water, that had brought them here after the rain.

Less than a quarter mile beyond the tank, Longarm could see the lights of a ranch house, this one not a soddy but an actual house of frame construction.

Longarm let the horses drink from the tank and lick at the salt a bit while he thought it over. Ahead in that house would be food and warmth and shelter.

Ahead in that house could also be another man with a shotgun who had been warned to watch out for strangers riding the country.

Ahead could be more danger than help.

If he had been alone, Longarm would not have hesitated. He would have ridden wide of the place and gone on to take his chances.

But behind him, Timmy Ryan continued to cling helplessly to the horn of his saddle, still shaken by chills, still burning with fever.

It would be scant help to save the kid from a hanging only to let him die of an ague.

"Come along, kid," Longarm said finally. "Let's go see if we can find ourselves a welcome." He gave the boy a grim smile. "Or not."

Chapter 15

Longarm stopped the horses in the yard directly in front of the doorway and hesitated for only a moment. But there was nothing to be gained from waiting. His decision had already been made. For the boy. If someone came outside now with a gun in hand there was nothing Deputy Long could do about it. He would not—could not—return any gunfire.

He cleared his throat, then loudly called out, "Hello the house! This is Deputy United States Marshal Custis Long with a prisoner. Hello the house."

He could hear movement from inside the place, but for a moment nothing happened. Then a crude curtain hung at a front window was cautiously pulled back a few inches, and a shadow darkened the corner of the window frame.

Longarm reached into his pocket for one of the last of his cheroots, struck a match, and lighted it.

Even when the tip of the cheroot was a glowing coal he continued to hold the match high, revealing himself fully to whoever was inside the house, both hands cupped around the matchstem. He let the match burn until the flame neared his fingers before he dropped it.

Only then was the door unbolted and allowed to swing open.

The muzzle of a small shotgun or large-bore rifle showed black in the lamplight at the door.

"Come ahead. Slow."

Longarm blinked. The voice was that of a woman or perhaps a young boy. It could be that the man of the house was waiting off to one side, ready to jump in if . . . But that made little sense. The curtains were undisturbed and hanging loose now. No one was watching from there. And it was damned unlikely that anyone could have slipped out a back window and gotten into the shadows without Longarm hearing. Not when taut nerves had his senses as finely honed as they were right now.

"Come ahead," the voice repeated.

"Right," Longarm said. "Slow and easy."

He stepped his horse forward, one pace at a time, Timmy Ryan's mount following.

He moved forward until he would be clearly visible in the light coming from inside the house, and only then stopped.

"I'm getting down now."

"All right."

He dismounted, still careful to move slowly, and reached for his wallet.

"Easy," the voice said. The speaker, who continued to hide at the doorjamb showing only the barrel of what Longarm could now see was an elderly Springfield musket of war vintage, sounded nervous.

"I'm getting my credentials, that's all."

"All right. But slow."

He pulled his hand back into view and flipped it open so the light caught the surface of his badge and gleamed brightly off it.

"Oh, Lordy."

There was a sob of relief from inside the house, and the muzzle of the heavy old .58 caliber musket sagged down toward the floor.

"Oh, Lordy," the voice repeated again. "I . . . I been so scared."

Longarm dropped his reins, leaving Ryan for the moment, and crossed the short distance that separated him from the house.

Just inside the place and leaning against the front wall as if for badly needed support was a young woman, hardly more than a girl, whose face was tear-tracked and pale. "I been . . . I been . . . thank God you ain't one o' them, Marshal. When I seen you ride in I was sure you was one o' them."

"It's all right now, miss. Everything is just fine now." He took the long-barreled Springfield from her weak, unresisting hands and propped the old frontloader against the wall, then turned her by the shoulders and guided her to a seat at the table that occupied most of the front room.

She tried to smile her thanks but was still too overwhelmed by as yet unfaded fears to bring it off.

"It's all right," he said again. "Will you mind if I leave you long enough to bring in my prisoner—he's a mighty sick youngster—and see to the horses?"

"I'll be . . ." She scrubbed at her eyes with both hands and ran the back of a wrist under her nose before she went on, "I'll be fine now, thank you. You go ahead and do what you need."

He went back outside to the horses and lifted Ryan down from the saddle. The boy tried to help but was too weak. Longarm draped Ryan's arm over his own broad shoulders and half carried the youngster into the house.

"Goodness!" The girl's teary eyes went wide when she saw the condition Ryan was in.

Her own recent fears forgotten now, she leaped up and helped Longarm support him.

"No," she ordered, taking charge now, "not to a chair. He needs a bed." She paused for a fraction of a second to

113

give a look toward a ladder leading to a loft overhead, then shook her head as if to herself and guided them toward one of the two small rooms at the back of the house. It was a bedroom, cluttered with heavy furnishings and masculine gear including a fancy saddle and a rack of carbines and shotguns on the side wall.

"We'll put him here," she said, pulling the covers back while Longarm lowered Ryan onto the welcome softness. She dropped to her knees to pull his boots off before she realized that Ryan was not wearing any.

Longarm laid the boy onto the mattress, and the girl quickly tugged the bedclothes up chin-high over him.

"I can see to him now," she said briskly. "You go tend the animals." There seemed nothing left of the limp, frightened girl who had been at the doorway only a minute or two earlier.

"Yes, ma'am," Longarm said with amusement. Give a young girl a chance to play mother and she was in her element, he guessed. This one sure seemed to be.

He hesitated a moment looking at the two of them, Ryan shivering under the covers and this suddenly competent girl hovering over him like a hen with a chick in need. He smiled.

On this closer inspection the girl was even younger than he had first thought. Mid-teens, he thought. She was a thin, rather plain little thing with lifeless brown hair pulled into a severe bun at the nape of her neck and a gray and faded shapeless dress hanging loose over a figure that probably was about as shapeless as the dress that covered it.

Yet she moved with calm assurance now, smoothing the pale hair back off Timmy Ryan's forehead while she checked to see if he was feverish, then turning with a nod to find Longarm still standing behind her.

"What are you waiting for? Get on with you now. I can tend him. You've your own things to do."

"Yes, ma'am," Longarm said again.

This time he left them alone and went back outside to unsaddle the horses, turn them loose in one of the pens close to the house, and rummage through the several sheds until he found some wild grass hay to feed them.

There was no windmill at the house, but a hand-dug well with a windlass and bucket was between the house and corrals. He drew and carried water until there was more than enough in a trough the horses could reach, then hung the saddles in one of the sheds and returned to the house.

He had taken his time with the choring, and now there was a hiss of steam coming from a kettle on the stove in the second back room, which turned out to be given to food storage and kitchen use.

The sight of so many cans and boxes of foodstuffs made his belly knot with hunger.

Both doors off the main room were open. Longarm could see Ryan lying under the bedding in the one room. In the other the girl was busy shaving fragments of beef into a pot.

She looked up and saw him standing there.

"I'll be needing water," she said. "Broths." Her knife blade snapped down against the cutting board. "He needs broth to begin with, then soup. You can bring me some water, and we'll get started with this."

"Yes, ma'am."

She sniffed impatiently. "Men! If he'd stayed in your care he'd be dead soon enough. Even a prisoner don't deserve that."

"No, ma'am."

"Get on now. Fetch me that water. Bucket's in the corner. Over there." She pointed with the blade of the knife, then went back to her work. "A full draw, if you please."

Longarm grinned at her and touched the brim of his hat to her.

Scared as she had been just a little while ago, all that was sure as hell behind them now.

Longarm made a beeline for the water pail she had pointed out to him and did as he was told.

• • •

Finally Longarm got a chance to sit down to some food. First the girl had insisted on filling Timmy Ryan with steaming hot beef broth and coffee laced syrupy thick with canned milk and brown sugar. Only when Ryan was sound asleep under practically every blanket and comforter in the house did she consent to fix something to ease the pains in Longarm's belly.

Hungry though he was, he ate sparingly at first, giving his stomach a chance to adjust to the presence of food again. Only when he was sure his system would accept it did he tuck into the cold biscuits, wild plum jam, and fried antelope steaks that she set out for him.

Later, feeling infinitely better although suddenly exhausted, he sat back in his chair and reached for the coffee she poured for him.

"You'll never know how much I appreciate that," he said with feeling. He cocked his head to one side and raised an eyebrow. "It occurs to me, miss, that I never quite got your name."

"Hannah," she told him. "Hannah Thompson."

"Then please accept my thanks, Hannah Thompson."

"No thanks necessary, Marshal. Believe me. Ever since we heard . . ." She shuddered and shook her head.

"Just what is it you're so worried about, miss? Or is it missus?" She was young, but it certainly was not impossible that she was the mistress of this household. Girls often tended to marry at an early age, particularly in such isolated country where women would be few and men needful of helpmates on their farms and ranches, the sort of help that could only be had from a wife.

"Miss," she told him. "My daddy homesteaded here while the railroad was still building west."

It was no wonder, then, that the place was so well established, with the frame house and collection of outbuildings. The railroad had been completed through Nebraska for some years.

Longarm nodded and took another swallow of his coffee. He thought about having another cheroot, but he had only two left, and there was no telling when he would be

116

able to get more. He'd been thinking for some time about cutting back on his smoking, but this was not exactly the way he had intended to do it.

"But you were asking about my worries? I thought you must be part of the hunt, you being a federal deputy and all. I mean . . ." Her eyes cut toward the side wall beyond which Timmy Ryan was sleeping.

Longarm shook his head. It was not exactly lying. Closer to the truth, in fact, than anyone else around here was likely to understand for the time being. "The boy in there is just a cowboy who got caught up in something that wasn't his fault. At least that's the way I see it. I got to regard him as a prisoner, anyhow, until a judge says I can turn him loose."

"I see. Then you must not know what's been happening around here," Hannah Thompson said.

"I'd appreciate it if you'd tell me."

The girl shuddered again. "It's awful, Marshal. Simply awful."

Longarm smiled at her over the rim of his cup. "Awful covers a lot of territory, Miss Thompson. Could you be a mite more particular about it?"

"Yes, of course." She sat straighter in her chair and smoothed her dress over her lap, obviously feeling much more herself now that she had the protection of the law under her roof. "You see, there were some killings down in Washington. They say a regular army of outlaws invaded the town and robbed practically everyone there. Shot down I don't know how many innocent people right there on the streets."

Longarm found it interesting but certainly not surprising how the tale had grown since the morning of the twin robberies. He said nothing about that, however.

"Anyway," she went on, "the leader of this gang actually volunteered to ride with the posse when the menfolk went out after them. And when the posse caught up with the gang, this leader pulled a gun on those poor possemen and shot his way clear, taking the murderers with him."

Longarm drank again quickly to hide the smile that was

pulling at his lips. Volunteered, had he? Shot his way clear with his fellow gang members, had he? Lordy, but this would be funny if it wasn't so damn serious. The notions that could get into people's heads . . .

"So of course the whole country's after them now. That's where my daddy is right now. He volunteered to ride with them soon as he got the word about it. I . . . I have to admit that I wasn't so keen on the idea of him going with them and leaving me alone here. But he said it shouldn't take long with so many men riding now, combing the country and knowing it better than this gang ever could. And it isn't like it was in the old days when there was Indian trouble to worry about." An old sadness dulled her eyes, but only for a moment. She recovered quickly. "That was what happened to my mama once when Daddy was off gathering beeves. I was just little then and I can't remember any of it except how it smelled where she hid me under some potato sacks in the cellar. The Sioux got her that time and burned the old house we had then, but Daddy rebuilt. And it isn't like that any more."

Longarm thought she sounded like she was trying to convince herself of that more than she was informing him. No wonder she had been so frightened when he showed up in her yard at night with her daddy away.

"Anyway, the men are all out looking for this gang. I just naturally assumed that you were part of the hunt for them."

Longarm grunted, not exactly answering her. He did not want to lie to her, but he did not want to raise needless questions either. "It sounds like they have everything under control without me," he said. "Have you heard if they've had any success so far?" He was thinking about Sam Dolan, dead those many miles behind now.

"No, but whoever they are had better watch out. The men of this country know how to fight. Those of them that weren't in the War have mostly had experience against Sioux raiders. They know how to handle themselves."

Longarm had to figure she was talking about the ranchers of the country. She damn sure couldn't mean the

118

posse members Sheriff Harlan Walker had led out of Washington.

"Well, you're safe enough now," he told her. He smiled. "For a meal as welcome as that one was, Hannah, I'd fight off a dozen gangs of raiders, red or white either one."

The girl blushed, accepting it as a compliment to her cooking and obviously liking the attention.

"Could I get you anything more, Marshal? Coffee? Or maybe another steak?"

"Thanks, but I'm full as a tick in a hound's ear. The only thing more you could do for me would be to call me Longarm. That's what my friends do. That and excuse me from the table now. I'm almighty tired."

"You can . . . Oh, dear, I hadn't thought about where you should sleep. I could make you a pallet in the bedroom by your prisoner if you like."

"No need for that. I can bed down out in the shed. Unless you're uncomfortable being under the same roof with Ryan."

"Is that his name?" She shook her head. "I doubt he will wake again until somebody shakes him out. I'm not worried about that, Marshal." She paused and smiled. "Longarm, I mean."

"I'll go on out to the shed then," Longarm said, rising. "If you get to worrying about anything in the night, just speak. I sleep light."

"Thank you." She stood and walked with him to the front door, holding onto his elbow while she did so. It was obvious that she trusted him completely, and he was glad it was he and Ryan who had chanced onto the place instead of the real gang of robbers. If they had showed up instead it would have been a matter of letting the fox loose in the henhouse for sure.

"Good night, Miss Hannah."

"Good night, Longarm." Her voice was a breathless whisper in the night. "I won't bolt the door. In case you need in for anything."

"Thanks."

He went out into the shed, his feet dragging with fatigue

119

now that his belly was full and he could relax for a bit. Behind him Hannah Thompson continued to stand in the lighted doorway until Longarm was out of sight. Only then did she swing the door closed and go back into the kitchen to tidy up before retiring.

Chapter 16

"Longarm."

He woke with a start from a sleep so sound that for a moment he did not remember where he was. It had been a long time since he had slept like that.

The sun was fully up, and Hannah Thompson was standing in the doorway of the ranch house across the yard with a mixing bowl in one hand and an apron covering her dress.

"Yes?" There had been no hint of alarm in her voice, so he sat on Ron Deal's bedroll and pulled his boots on before he went out to see what she wanted.

"Breakfast in ten minutes."

"Thanks." He had filled up the night before, but food still sounded almighty good to him.

Hannah disappeared back inside the house, leaving the door standing open. Longarm went to the well to draw water for his morning toilet and found the outhouse.

Ten minutes later he tapped lightly on the doorframe to let her know he was coming in, then went to the bedroom door to check on Timmy Ryan. The kid was still asleep and looked like he hadn't moved since the last time Longarm saw him. He was no longer shivering, though, and his color was much better.

Hannah appeared at Longarm's side, wiping her hands on a dish towel. "I hadn't the heart to wake him yet. I think he needs rest more than anything right now. When he wakes up I'll give him some mush and milk."

"You have a cow?" Longarm was surprised. Eastern notions notwithstanding, damn few working ranches wanted to be bothered with the nuisance of milking. They raised beef breeds and generally looked down on dairy cattle.

"Of course not," Hannah said. "We buy canned milk like everybody else." She sounded almost indignant at his notion that the Thompsons might keep a milker around.

"Sorry." Longarm followed her into the kitchen. She set a groaning table for him but ate very little herself. Longarm felt no such reluctance. He had several days of short rations to make up for and was willing to close the gap as quickly as possible.

Hannah was not very talkative this morning, he noticed. In between birdsized bites she sat with her hands in her lap and her eyes down. He began to wonder if he had done something to offend her.

The period of awkwardness was interrupted by the sound of movement in the next room. Hannah was away from the table before Longarm had time to move. She went into the bedroom and came back a moment later. "He wants you to help him with something. The . . . uh . . . the receptacle is under the bed." She flushed with discomfort at having come so close to mentioning an unmentionable subject, then busied herself at the stove while Longarm went to assist Timmy Ryan behind the closed bedroom door.

The kid was still weak, but he looked one hell of a lot better than he had when they pulled into the Thompson place. Longarm gave him the help he needed and in a low voice informed Ryan of the situation.

"Better if you don't exactly say anything about the kind of trouble you happen to be in here, not even about Dolan. You understand? No point in inviting hysterics or worse."

"I won't say nothing, Marshal," Ryan whispered. The kid shivered and for a moment Longarm thought the fevers were coming back on him, but it was the memory of Sam Dolan lying in another ranch yard instead. Ryan would want no repeat of that, and Longarm did not blame him.

"I c'n ride now, Marshal. Any time you want t' head out, I can."

"We'll see," Longarm said.

He had no doubt that Ryan meant it. The kid would do his best in the saddle and might even be able to manage it now that he had some food in him to help rebuild his strength.

Still, it occurred to Longarm that a man leaves no tracks when he is standing still. With the countryside under armed alert, it just might be wise to stick where they were for the time being, to give the search parties time to become discouraged. Longarm had never known a rancher or a farmer who lacked work to keep him busy, and none of the men in the search would want to stay away from their homes for long. It just might not be a bad idea to hole up here for a while, at least until the first flush of passions of fear and rumor subsided, and then go in some safety to get the mess straightened out.

It did not bother him at all that so much effort was being expended on the false search for him and for Timmy Ryan.

For one thing, a search directed at the two of them might easily blunder into the real robbers.

For another, this business was not part of his federal jurisdiction. If Sheriff Harlan Walker wanted to make a damn fool of himself and every other man in Nebraska, it really was no sweat off Longarm's brow.

Longarm carried the thundermug out to the backhouse to empty it. When he came back, the girl was in with Ryan, spoon-feeding him mush and milk. She had him propped up against several pillows with his arms under the

123

chin-high covers and was handling the spoon for him.

Longarm went into the kitchen and helped himself to another cup of coffee. When the girl returned to join him there he grinned at her. "I'd say Timmy is making the most out of you caring for him, making you feed him like that."

Hannah gave Longarm a sharp look. "I tried letting him use the spoon himself. He was so weak he couldn't handle it without spilling everything."

Ready to ride, was he? It looked like the kid had more nerve than sense.

"Would it put you out if we were to stay here for another day or so, miss?"

"Hannah," she corrected. "And I would be grateful for your protection if you would stay, Longarm."

Longarm fingered his chin. His razor was back in Washington, and Ron Deal had not packed one along on the posse run. "Then I'll thank you for the hospitality, Hannah, and accept it with pleasure," he told her.

She beamed with pleasure, then dropped her eyes away from his and blushed before she spoke. "I . . . uh, I could let you use Daddy's razor if you'd like."

Just why that should cause her to blush he couldn't figure, but it was an offer he was not going to let slide. Having half an unplanned beard was not comfortable, and he was needing to trim his moustache. He smoothed it unconsciously and Hannah blushed again.

Damn strange girl, Longarm thought.

He stood, towering over her, and stretched, a lean, darkly handsome man. He ran a hand over the stubble on his cheek and smiled down at her, bringing yet another flush of bright red to her otherwise pale cheeks. "A shave would be real welcome, Hannah. Thanks."

"Do you . . . I could shave you if you'd like. I do that sometimes for Daddy. He has just an awful time getting under the sides of his jaw here." Her hand crept up and touched him lightly high on the neck. He could feel that for some reason she was trembling just a little.

"That won't be necessary, but I thank you just the same."

Hannah bobbed her head nervously, then hurried out of the room to return a moment later with a leather case of razors, a strop, and a mug of shaving soap. "There's a mirror . . ."

"I know. I saw it. Thanks." He took the shaving gear from her outstretched hands—she was holding them out in his general direction but was not meeting his eyes for some reason—and thanked her again. Then he went around to the back of the house, where the wash basin and mirror were.

He was wondering if it would be any trouble to get some hot water from her. A bath would be mighty welcome after several days on the dodge.

He began to whistle a gay tune while he shaved, and after a bit he could hear Hannah in the kitchen humming along with his tune.

Damn strange girl, he thought again.

Longarm thought the game was up early that afternoon. He and Hannah had just finished their dinner. Timmy Ryan had already been fed and was sleeping soundly in Hannah's father's bed. While the girl was washing the dishes, Longarm took the pail out to the well, intending to refill the reservoir built into the side of the stove.

He walked outside just in time to see a rider coming in. Quickly he set the bucket down at the front door and went back inside to warn Hannah.

"Rider," he told her in a low voice. "You might want to take a quick look and see if it's anyone you know."

She probably saw him check the Colt at his waist to make sure the big .44 was loose in its holster. He had no mind to fire at any honest posseman from Washington or any other town. But it was not impossible that the real gang of robbers could stumble onto the Thompson place, just as Longarm and Ryan had done. This one man could be an outrider checking up on things before the rest of the gang came in.

Hannah grabbed a dish towel and hurried to the front

door, wringing her hands in the towel as much as drying them.

She looked worried until she reached the opening. Then she relaxed visibly.

"It's only Charlie."

"Charlie?"

"Charlie Tweed," she explained. "He works for the Three Spoons, Mr. Cuthbert's place north of here." She blushed. "Charlie thinks he's sweet on me."

"I see." Longarm forced a smile that he did not at all feel. Charlie Tweed might be harmless as a titmouse to Hannah Thompson, but a wrong word from him could put a hangman's noose around Timmy Ryan's neck. Or a bullet into Custis Long's back. Longarm would not find either of those the more agreeable for knowing that it was only a mistake.

As a precaution Longarm crossed the room and pulled the bedroom door closed so the visitor would not see Ryan, then returned to the door to wait with Hannah while Charlie Tweed rode into the yard and tied his horse to a corral rail.

"Hello, Charlie."

"M-m-miss Hannah." Tweed blushed and swept his hat off, fumbling it from hand to hand awkwardly.

"Well, come inside if you have to, Charlie. We just finished our dinner, but there's some left over I can set out for you."

Tweed had had eyes only for Hannah, but at the word "we" he looked past her and saw the tall, handsome deputy standing there. He said nothing, but Longarm could see that the youngster did not like having someone else there.

He used the brim of his hat to slap some dust off his britches and stamped his feet repeatedly on the wooden planks of the porch before he entered the house.

When Hannah turned to go back to the kitchen, Tweed gave Longarm a frown.

Longarm could not decide if Hannah was unaware of Charlie Tweed's feelings in the matter, or if the girl was enjoying them so much that she pretended not to notice.

Either way, it was an uncomfortable position for Longarm.

Before it could get any worse, Longarm stuck his hand out to shake with the cowboy. "Long," he said. "Deputy United States marshal out of Denver. I was passing through and stopped for a meal. And you would be . . .?"

Tweed hesitated only for a moment. Then he smiled and shook while he introduced himself.

Hannah Thompson was no great beauty, being plain and thin and years too young, but Charlie Tweed was an out-and-out loser. When the good looks were passed out, Charlie must have been off getting a second helping of teeth. He was bucktoothed and nearly jawless so that he looked something like a beaver, and although he could not have been past his mid-twenties he was already well on his way to being bald. What hair he had looked like it hadn't been washed since the last time he fell in a creek, and that must not have happened for a year or so.

"Please to meet you," Longarm lied pleasantly.

"Yeah . . . uh, same here."

Helluva dashing suitor Hannah had here, Longarm thought, but he continued to smile.

"What brings you this way, Charlie?" Hannah asked as she set out the leftovers from dinner and a clean plate and cup.

"I been riding with the posse," Charlie said proudly, implying in his tone of voice that it had been rough and dangerous work. He sat to the table and began shoveling food into his mouth, talking around the huge bites and hardly slowing his pace at all while he spoke. "Mr. Cuthbert, he wanted me to swing up t' the ponds seein' as we got some rain, make sure there's nothing bogged, then I can meet them agin if they ain't caught their men yet. Thought I'd best swing by here an' make sure you was all right whilst I was goin' by, Hannah. I was worryin' about you. Told your daddy I'd stop. Told him I'd check on his cows too if I seen any. Druther be with the boys on the chase, o' course, but a man's got t' do what he's got t' do."

Longarm watched Charlie Tweed's performance with something close to awe, truly amazed that a man could talk so fast and eat so much all at one and the same time. Flecks of food spattered and flew in all directions while Tweed talked and ate, but Tweed took no notice of that and never slowed for a second.

"Naturally," Tweed nattered on, "I was frettin' about you being alone here. Gave me a start when I seen there was a stranger with you. But your daddy will feel better about it knowin' it's a marshal staying with you." He cut his eyes toward Longarm. That last had been more question than comment.

"Oh, I won't be staying," Longarm said, knowing it was what Tweed was hoping to hear. "I'm just passing through. Miss Thompson has been telling me something about the troubles down this way. Not that it is a federal matter. I wouldn't have jurisdiction here unless your local law asked me to come in on the case, and they seem to have things well in hand without that."

"Now that's the truth," Tweed said. "We got us a good bunch o' boys ridin'. Ever'body well armed and full on the prod. Won't anybody get past us, no sirree. 'Most every man in the country is out b' now."

"So I understand," Longarm said. "Any luck so far?"

"Some. Bill Harris down toward Fairo got one of 'em the other night. They tried to pull a raid on his place, but Harris was waitin' for 'em. The rest got away, but Harris shot this one right in the chest. Da... excuse me, Miss Hannah... darn shame Harris only had birdshot in his gun. Didn't kill the sonuvabuck, but he's in powerful bad shape. They carried him down to Fairo and have him in the jail there."

Charlie Tweed couldn't know it, but that was the best news Longarm had had in quite a long time. So Dolan was still alive in a jail cell. Ryan would be glad to hear it too.

"The rest of 'em," Tweed sputtered on, still stuffing his face while he talked, "we about got cornered down south o' here."

Longarm suppressed a smile. The fifty-fifty dodge they had tried among those cattle tracks had worked, then.

128

Worked so well that the searchers believed their quarry was run to earth down toward the rails.

"That's why I got t' hurry. Got t' get th' chores done up this way in time t' get back down there. I wanta be in on it when they take 'em." His expression hardened, and if he had had a jaw it would have been firmly set. "They didn't give no quarter in Washington. We don't figure to give none back when we catch 'em."

Tweed reached down and fingered the chipped and battered grips of an old cap and ball Remington revolver that had been converted to cartridge use at some time in the past. He tried to look tough and menacing, undoubtedly for Hannah's benefit.

Longarm reached for the cup of coffee Hannah had given him. No quarter. It was no more than he had expected, but still it was not a pleasant prospect. And not only for himself and Ryan if they should be caught before Longarm could get them to a place of sanity.

The worst part of it was that the searchers might stumble on any innocent party passing through this country and shoot when they should have been asking pointed questions.

Damn them anyhow, Longarm thought. Someone needed to put a stop to this.

In the meantime, Longarm still had to worry about Charlie Tweed. Another two days or so and the homely cowboy would be back with the posse. He was sure to talk about the stranger he had seen at the Thompson place. If there was anyone from the original Washington posse listening, a description would be a dead giveaway.

Tweed, oblivious to Longarm now, was making moon eyes toward Hannah and stammering something about his concern for her welfare while her father was away and how he was glad she did not need his protection at the moment. At the same time he continued to devastate the leftovers Hannah had put in front of him. Apparently he did not intend to quit until the table was clear of everything edible.

When Tweed finally got done eating, there was nothing

left within reach and the coffee pot was down to the grounds. He gave Longarm a pointed look and did some hemming and hawing.

Longarm took the hint and excused himself, reaching for his hat. He went outside.

So far, he was pleased to realize, no mention had been made of the ailing "prisoner" in Thompson's bedroom.

The fewer strangers in the country Tweed knew to talk about, the less risk there was of anyone becoming suspicious about the visitors at the Thompson ranch.

Longarm walked out by the corral and leaned on the top rail. He lighted his last cheroot, intending to savor only a few puffs from it and then put it out and save the rest for later.

Tweed was inside alone with Hannah for only a minute or two. When he came back outside he was in a hurry, and Longarm thought there was a suspiciously red place on his cheek. Either he was blushing about something or he had just gotten the hell slapped out of him.

Apparently little Hannah was quite capable of taking care of herself.

Tweed did not stop to pass the time of day with Longarm. The cowboy jammed his hat onto his head and mounted in a hurry, riding away toward the north with no more than a curt nod for a farewell.

Longarm could not claim that he was exactly sorry to see the Three Spoons rider go. He took a last drag on the cheroot and carefully pried the burning coal off the tip of it. He crushed the coal underfoot, blew through the now extinguished cheroot so stale smoke would not affect the taste when he relighted the thing, and tucked the shortened stick of tobacco back into his pocket.

Things would be a lot easier if Timmy Ryan would hurry and get well enough to ride again, Longarm thought.

He went back inside to check on the boy, wishing there was something more he could do.

Chapter 17

Longarm leaned back against a pile of Thompson's hay and crossed his booted ankles. If he had had another cheroot this would have been a fine time for a smoke. His belly was full, Ryan was sleeping as usual, and Hannah Thompson had blown out the lamps in the house. It was a good time to do some thinking. Certainly he had done nothing during the day to make him tired.

He was not much for belaboring worries that were beyond his power to control, so there was no point in fretting about what would happen after Ryan could move again. Time enough to think about that when it happened.

Instead he was thinking further down the road. To his return to Denver and what he would tell Billy Vail.

He had made up his mind to resign his badge. Hadn't he?

Well, pretty much. But the truth was—and wasn't that

131

damned strange—he was not feeling as depressed as he had been before this mess started.

A man ought to look at things the other way around, he reasoned. After all, a few days ago he had been employed, and reasonably successful at what he did—at least the way others seemed to see it—with money in his pockets and time on his hands.

Yet his spirit had been low enough to slide under a snake's belly and the only thing he had been able to accomplish was to get himself stinking drunk.

Now he was being hunted by a clear majority of the male population of southern Nebraska, probably with a price on his head. And he was starting to feel better.

Didn't make any sense.

Yet, hell, if he'd had a bottle handy he would have welcomed a drink right now. That and a smoke, and the truth was that he would actually be feeling pretty good.

Man can be an awfully irrational critter, Longarm thought.

He wasn't even quite so positive now that he was going to write out that letter when he got back to Denver. Maybe yes, maybe no. It would depend on how things felt when he got there.

Across the yard he heard the house door open, and then there was the sound of footsteps on the gravel. Hannah was coming over to the shed where Longarm's bed was made out.

He checked to see that he was properly buttoned and tucked, then stood to greet her.

"Are you all right?"

She jumped, a hand going to her mouth. "Oh! I didn't see you in the shadows there."

"Sorry." He stepped into the moonlight and smiled down at her. "You *are* all right, aren't you?"

"Yes. Yes, of course. I just . . . I brought you something."

He could not be sure, but he thought she might be blushing again. The light was too poor for him to tell for certain.

132

"Here." She thrust her fist forward. "These are daddy's. I noticed, a little while ago that is, I noticed you were smoking a stub. I thought you might like some of these."

"Why, thank you."

He accepted the cigars she gave him. They were crooks, cheap and harsh, but smokes. He smelled one of them. The tobacco had been rum-cured to impart an artificial sweetness where the natural flavors were lacking. A rum crook would not be his smoke of choice, but under the circumstances they were damned well welcome.

"Thank you," he repeated.

The girl bobbed her head but made no move to return to the house. She began to shiver, and he hoped she was not catching whatever it was that laid Timmy Ryan low.

"You're chilly," he said.

"Yes." She kept her eyes down and still did not move toward the house.

"Would you like to go inside?" he prompted.

Longarm had been thinking in terms of the house, but instead Hannah went into the shed and helped herself to a seat on Longarm's bedroll. He joined her but remained standing, not wanting to imply that he would compromise her.

After a moment Hannah stood also. She moved closer to him, eyes down, hands wringing nervously together.

"Is something wrong, Hannah?" he asked gently.

"No," she said quickly. Then, "Yes." She gave him a brief look of utter hopelessness. "I don't know."

"Do you want to tell me about it?"

"Yes."

He stood waiting, but she said nothing. To give her time to collect her thoughts, he nipped off the end of one of the rum crooks and took his time about lighting it.

In the flare of the match he could see that Hannah was pale and trembling. She acted like a fawn ready to bolt from danger but rooted motionless by curiosity. Or by fear.

He could not think of anything she might be afraid of. No one had come near the place since Tweed left that afternoon. Unless Ryan . . . But that was not likely. The boy

133

was still much too weak to be giving her that kind of trouble, even if he was the sort to be otherwise so inclined, and Longarm doubted that from what he knew of the kid.

"Is it anything I can help with?" he asked.

She nodded briskly but continued to keep her eyes down away from his. "Yes." The word came out as a barely audible whisper.

"I'll do anything I can. I hope you know that."

She nodded again but remained silent.

After a moment she turned to face away from him. Her hands fluttered nervously in front of her. She looked very small and vulnerable standing in front of him.

Without warning she gave a loud moan of frustration.

While her back was turned she had been fumbling at the buttons on the front of her dress.

Now, trapped somewhere between eagerness and panic, she pulled the shapeless garment off her shoulders and almost in the same motion turned, allowing the dress to fall to the ground around her bare ankles.

She was wearing nothing under the dress.

She stood before him, naked, pathetically thin, defenseless. Mutely offering herself to him. Still unable to meet his eyes in her fear of rejection.

Longarm swallowed. Hard.

Lordy, she was . . . what . . . fourteen? fifteen? Just on the fringes of womanhood, but not yet there.

There was no question in his mind that she was yet a virgin.

Some things a man could do. Some he could convince himself it would be all right to do. Others were beyond the pale. For him to take this girl now would be to harm, perhaps to destroy her.

Yet to reject her out of hand would be even worse. That he could not do either.

Careful not to look at her half-formed body, Longarm stepped forward. Hannah was trembling. She stood as if poised between flight and passion.

Gently, very gently, Longarm cupped her chin in his

palm and tipped her head up until he could see into her eyes. He smiled.

"You are lovely," he said. "And I'm honored that you would want to be with me."

Hannah looked like she was about to cry. The tears welled full in her eyes but did not spill out. They pooled shimmering there in the thin bit of moonlight that reached inside the shed.

Slowly, so as not to frighten her, Longarm bent his lips to hers and kissed her.

Her lips were cold with her fears, and she was inexperienced even at this.

He put an arm around her thin shoulders. She felt as light and fragile as a bird. He kissed her again, and this time she moaned aloud and pressed herself to him.

Longarm pulled back away from her. He moved only a little, but it was enough for her to feel, enough to confuse her. She looked up at him, and now the tears overflowed and trailed down her cheeks.

"What . . . ?"

"Shhhhh." He silenced her with a touch of a fingertip to her lips, then kissed her again chastely.

"I don't understand."

He smiled at her and hugged her. "You are a lovely young woman, Hannah Thompson."

"I know better'n that, Longa—"

"Shhhh. You are. Don't you ever think otherwise. And if I was free to be with you, Hannah, I'd be proud to claim you for my own. Proud to have you on my arm in the finest spots in Denver." He smiled and kissed her again. "And that's the natural truth."

"But . . . ?"

"But I'm a married man, sweet Hannah."

"Oh, goshamighty!" She sounded horrified.

"I wish I'd told you sooner," Longarm said. "I would have if I'd suspected. You see, I just didn't think it was so obvious that I was attracted to you. I'm awful sorry if I gave you a wrong impression. I thought I was hiding it better than that. But I care for you too much to do you wrong, Hannah Thompson, and in truth I wouldn't be willing to do my wife wrong neither. I hope you understand. I hope you'll forgive me."

"Oh, Lordy, Longarm, I didn't know."

"Will you forgive me? Please?"

She nodded solemnly, and Longarm bent to kiss her lightly on the lips again.

"Thank you," he said.

Hannah blinked back the last of her tears and wiped the back of her hand over her eyes and then beneath her nose. She sniffled loudly.

Longarm stroked her cheek with the ball of his thumb, then turned away.

He could hear the girl scrambling quickly back into her dress.

Before she could have had time to button it she moved close behind him and pressed her cheek against his back, her skinny arms wrapping tight around his waist.

She hugged him with a fierce, sudden strength. But only for a moment. Then she was gone, running back toward the house without another word.

Longarm grinned into the night and took a deep, satisfying pull on the rum crook she had brought out to him.

In truth, he was rather proud of himself. She'd seemed to believe him. Likely *wanted* to believe him. It let them both get out of the situation feeling good about themselves.

The girl hadn't been harmed in body or spirit, either one.

Longarm grinned to himself some more.

Why, hell, she'd just done him a powerful favor too, if one she couldn't know she had accomplished.

Right now, Custis Long was feeling better about himself than he had in an awfully long time past.

He inhaled some of the acrid smoke of the crook and kicked his boots off. He suspected he would be getting a good night's sleep.

• • •

Longarm woke up feeling better than he had in . . . He gave it some active consideration and couldn't come up with so much as a guess. Whatever, it had been an awfully long time.

He bounced onto his feet, stretched hugely, yawned once, and got dressed. It was just coming dawn and the sky to the east was pale. Farther to the west the few patches of scattered cloud were streaked pink and gold.

By the time Longarm had visited the outhouse, washed, and shaved, Hannah had the stove going, and he could smell bacon frying.

"*Good* morning," he said cheerfully as he went in to join her.

"You look . . . you look nice this morning," the girl said timidly.

"So do you." He bent and gave her a friendly peck on the forehead, then took a chair. The coffee had begun to boil but was not quite ready yet.

"You aren't mad at me?" she asked.

Longarm smiled. "Never."

"Good." She smiled too now. "Breakfast in five minutes."

"I'll check on our patient while you finish in here."

Hannah nodded absently, busy with her cooking, and Longarm went to look in on Ryan.

The young fellow stirred when the door opened, and after a moment his eyes came open.

"G'morning, Marshal." He still sounded weak. "I'm holding you up. But I c'n ride today. I know I can."

"Uh-huh." Longarm pulled the boy's covers higher under his chin. The sheets were damp with sweat. Ryan had had fever during the night again. He was far from being able to ride, even if he refused to admit to the fact.

"Don't worry about it," Longarm told him. "I'm gonna leave you here with Miss Thompson while I go and do something about this stupidity before some more innocent folks get hurt."

That was not something he had consciously planned. He did not realize himself what he intended until he heard

137

himself tell Timmy Ryan about it.

But, damn it, it was the best course. Those fools were roaming the countryside with guns in their hands and blood in their eyes, and any stray soul who crossed their path was apt to get blown to kingdom come.

If Harlan Walker and Ron Deal hadn't sense enough to see that danger and do something about it, Custis Long would just have to.

This had gone far enough.

Over breakfast Longarm told Hannah Thompson the truth about himself and Ryan. The whole truth this time. As he had hoped, the girl had become their ally by now.

Longarm suspected, in fact, that she would go along with him if he told her he and the boy had just come down off a ladder to the moon. Not that he intended to test that notion. The truth was good enough.

"But I think that's just awful, Longarm!" she exclaimed.

"No worse than a lot o' things that happen to innocent folks when somebody has a mad on. Just lucky I happened to be there an' could do something about it."

"But that poor boy! And his friend!" She looked toward the bedroom door, her eyes wide with sympathy and tenderness.

Longarm hid a smile. Little Hannah was feeling a woman's yearnings—the nesting instinct, some called it— and it would not surprise him a whole hell of a lot if she very soon began to shift her thoughts and attentions to Timmy Ryan, now that she knew Longarm was unavailable.

There were worse things that could happen to either of them, if that was the way it turned out. He wished them well.

"You wouldn't mind me leaving him here?" Longarm asked. "You might have to lie to protect him if your friend Tweed or your dad or somebody should return before I get back."

"Huh. Just let anybody try an' put a hand on him while he's under my roof. Just let 'em try it!"

Longarm grinned at her. "Sounds to me like he'll be as safe here as he would be in his own bed down in Texas."

"Safer," Hannah assured him.

"You are a fine woman, Hannah Thompson."

"Thank you, Custis Long." This time she neither blushed nor looked away. She kept her head high and accepted the compliment with good grace. He liked to see that in her.

"Then if you don't need me for anything . . .?"

"Go on. You have work t' do and so have I."

Longarm lighted one of her father's rum crooks and went outside with the smelly thing, thinking as he walked.

He would want to take both horses. A riderless spare could be handy if it came to a chase. And he would want to borrow some food from Hannah, just in case it was needed.

He could head down toward this Fairo that Charlie Tweed had spoken of.

But Washington was where it had started. Washington was where he likely could find Walker and Deal to end it.

Straight at Washington was the way he would ride.

By the time he returned to the house, Hannah already had a burlap bag packed for him with biscuits, cold meat, canned peaches, and a little coffee.

"Good luck to you, Hannah Thompson."

She sniffed impatiently. "Go along now, Longarm. I shall have things under control here. You just worry about what you have t' do."

"Yes, ma'am." He winked at her, kissed her briefly on the cheek, and turned away.

Chapter 18

He spotted someone's midday fire some twenty-odd miles southwest of the Thompson place and immediately altered his line of travel. Not away from it this time, but directly toward it.

Half an hour later he dropped over a ridge to find nearly a dozen men preparing to break their noon camp. When Longarm came into sight several of them reached for rifles or carbines. The rest stood watching his approach with suspicion.

Longarm rode up to the remains of the fire and dismounted with a curt nod. He picked up the coffee pot that was sitting at the edge of the flaky coals and ash left by burned manure and asked, "Anybody got a cup I can use?"

"Who the hell are you?" someone demanded. The man had an unkempt moustache that should have been a nuisance at mealtime and was holding an early model Sharps carbine in his hands. Despite the belligerence in his voice, though, he did not raise the muzzle of the carbine.

"Deputy United States marshal," Longarm responded. "Denver district. Do you have a cup or not?"

The man blinked. "Uh, sure. Just a second." He had already been returning his eating tools to his saddlebags. Now he unfastened the straps on one side of the rig and produced a tin cup.

Longarm thanked him and poured coffee for himself. It was weaker than he liked, but hot enough. He ignored the men around him, who were giving each other uncertain but silent looks, as if each wanted to challenge his presence here but no one quite knew how to go about it.

Longarm finished his coffee, returned the cup to its owner, and produced his wallet. "You haven't asked, but you should have." He showed them the badge, and there was a general air of relaxation around the smouldering fire.

"We . . . well, you know what's been going on around here," the man with the moustache said. "You understand."

"I know some of it," Longarm said sternly. "Enough to know that a bunch of people are making damn fools of themselves. Why don't you tell me your side of it."

There was another exchange of nervous glances. Longarm folded his arms across his chest and stared grim-faced back at them. He let them stew under the accusation that was in his eyes and waited for someone to speak.

Eventually it was a middle-aged man with gray hair and a good bit of belly who spoke for them.

"This is a manhunt, Marshal," the man said. Longarm suspected he would be a ranch owner, not a hand.

"Witch hunt, more like it. But you go ahead, mister . . . ?"

"Gus Partee," the rancher admitted. "But you got no right to—"

"We'll get into a discussion of rights later," Longarm snapped. "Right now you're telling me why there are people waving guns and showing ropes all over this part of the country. Remember?"

Partee and the others didn't like that, which was just the

way Longarm wanted it. He wanted to put them on the defensive and keep them there.

Partee looked toward the others in the group as if seeking approval before he went on. He gave Longarm pretty much the same garbled account that Charlie Tweed had been told, the major difference being that he had heard Sam Dolan was killed in the "raid" at the Harris place.

Longarm had been looking at Partee. Now he swung his eyes toward the man standing next to the rancher. "You."

"Me?"

"That's right. You. What would you have done if somebody rode up to your place in the night?"

The man hesitated only for a moment. Then his expression firmed. "I'd've done the same thing Bill Harris done, Marshal. I'd've blowed the son of a bitch out of the saddle so fast—"

"Exactly," Longarm snapped. "That is exactly what you would have done. Same thing if some old boy came up to your camp tonight. You'd blow him right out of his saddle." Longarm spat on the ground with an expression of disgust. "What would you have done last week if somebody rode up to your fire or showed at your door? I'll tell you what you'd have done, by damn. You'd have told him to light and set, and you'd have got out the coffee pot for him. But what'd you do when I came along just now? 'Bout half of you reached for your guns. And the other half was ready to. Did I get an invitation? Did anybody offer me a cup of coffee? Hell, no. You were all ready to blow holes in my belly if I coughed wrong. Well, I want you to think about something now.

"What if the old boy you blew out of his saddle was just some paid-off hand riding down from the Dakotas?

"What if he was a federal peace officer? Or a surveyor? Or some other poor soul with every right to go his way in peace?"

No one answered, and now no one was willing to meet Longarm's accusing eyes either. Some of the men fidgeted with their gear. Most just stood there and stared down toward their boot toes.

"I'm breaking this party up," Longarm said. "This one and all the rest that are out on this witch hunt."

"We got a right—"

"You got a right to a fair trial if harm comes to innocent folks," Longarm returned angrily. "That right I'll personally guarantee you. And personally see to it that you sit behind bars until you get that fair trial too. D'you understand me?"

No one seemed inclined to answer.

"Do you understand me?"

"Yes," someone grudgingly said. There was a murmur of agreement after the first man spoke.

"Now go home. All of you. Leave this work to those as know what they're doing. Go on. Now."

There was a slow shuffle of movement toward the horses. Only Partee stayed where he was.

"We were just trying..."

"I know what you were trying to do," Longarm said, more softly this time. "I know what you were trying to do, and I don't blame you for it. It's just..." Longarm raised a hand, then let it drop again. "Go home," he said gently.

"Yes, sir," Partee said. The rancher turned and joined the others in his group.

Longarm stayed to kick the fire apart while the men of the posse scattered and rode slowly off in several directions heading, Longarm hoped, back to their homes or their work.

Longarm found and broke up another posse of eight men later that afternoon. This second bunch was not so serious about it as the first had been. They had brought more liquor than ammunition on the manhunt and seemed only mildly disappointed to be told to go home.

"If you say so, Marshal," the self-appointed leader of the crowd told him pleasantly enough. He looked to be a farmer, judging by his clothing and clodhopper shoes.

"It would be a good idea, Jensen."

Olaf Jensen took another pull from his bottle, wiped the neck, and offered it to Longarm, who declined. Longarm turned toward his horse. The men in Jensen's group were already talking about heading to town for a blow-out before they went back to their homes.

"Say, Marshal."

"Yes?" Longarm asked as he mounted.

"What you was tellin' us about? I think maybe, I don't know for sure you understand, but I think maybe you ought t' drift over toward Fat Woman Creek."

"Why is that, Jensen?"

The farmer turned toward a youngster no older than Timmy Ryan, who had been silent since Longarm found them.

"Tell the man what you told us earlier, Petey," Jensen said.

"Do I have to?"

"I think you should."

Petey hemmed and hawed some before he spit it out. "What I heard from another boy I run into this afternoon, Marshal," he said finally, "was that there's fixing t' be a hanging over on the Fat Woman tonight. That some of the boys cotched part o' the gang and are fixing t' do them before ol' Walker gets wind of it and wants t' waste time with a trial."

"Jesus!" Longarm blurted. "That's exactly what I've been afraid of here. Where is this Fat Woman Creek?"

There was no answer.

"Is that where you were all going when I stopped you?" Longarm demanded.

Reluctantly, Petey and the rest nodded.

"Then I suggest—"

"I'll take you," Jensen cut in. "No point in all of us going."

"All right."

The rest of the bunch split up, with no talk this time about partying in town before going home. Olaf Jensen led off toward the northwest, with Longarm riding close beside him.

The two riders dropped down into the shallow valley of the Fat Woman just before dark. The bottom was choked

145

with crackwillow and plum, and here and there a few straggly cottonwoods stood in a bend or curve. Longarm guessed the stream did not carry water the year around, but there was some running in it now, probably as a result of the recent rains.

"Downstream is where they ought to be gathered," Jensen said.

"You'd best pray they haven't gotten to the hanging part of the fun yet," Longarm told him.

"I already been, Marshal."

Longarm nodded and bumped his horse into a lope.

They saw the meeting place well before they reached it. It was dark by then, and a huge bonfire had been built with the luxury of actual firewood.

More than a score of men were gathered close around the flames, and there were at least as many bottles as there were men available to empty them.

Hell of a posse, Longarm thought sourly as he and Jensen dismounted at the picket rope that had been strung for the occasion.

A ring of fire-blackened stones showed that this was a commonly used meeting site in the area, probably a favored camping place during roundups or hunting excursions.

"Where's the rest of your boys, Olaf?" someone asked when Jensen came into the firelight.

Jensen shrugged and looked back over his shoulder. Longarm stepped into view beside him, tall and stern and bitterly accusing.

"This here is a U.S. marshal, boys. He's been thinking there might not be justice bein' done here tonight."

A man who was squatting beside the fire with a rope in his hands barked a grunt of dissent. "Justice? This here is exactly what justice is all about, mister. Eye for an eye, tooth for a tooth. Man kills his fellow man, he's got to expect to be kilt in return for it."

"I agree," Longarm said. "That's what courts of law are for. But first they make sure they've got the killer. Where is this prisoner of yours?"

"Prisoners," someone else corrected. "Three of 'em. It's the rest o' the gang, Marshal. Caught fair and square. There was them three that got away from the first posse Sher'f Walker took out, and now we got the rest of 'em."

"So you say." Longarm took out a rum crook, bit the tip off it, and lighted it. "Bring them out where I can see them."

The man who was fiddling with the rope looked like he wanted to balk, but someone else said, "Hell, yes. We got nothing to be ashamed of here."

Someone left the circle of light and a minute later returned herding a trio of short, dark-haired men who had their hands tied behind them. All three of the prisoners wore bright-colored shirts, grease-stained trousers and short boots.

Despite the predicament they were in, the bound prisoners carried themselves with no show of fear, looking boldly into the eyes of their captors. They were guarded by four men with shotguns, but chose to ignore the guards.

"Any of you fellows speak English?" Longarm asked.

"They don't say nothing at all," the man with the rope said, standing now. "Bold as brass, they are. Smart sons of bitches. They know they're caught, but they ain't said a word since we took 'em."

Longarm silenced the fool with a cutting look and repeated his question.

The prisoner on the left took a step forward and shook his head. He said something in a language Longarm did not understand, but it was one he had heard a time or two before.

The prisoner held himself erect, with his chin up and his gaze direct.

The man was afraid. Longarm was sure of that. Any sane man would be, given the mood and the guns and ropes that were in evidence here. But he had too much pride and dignity to let it show. He might hang if he had to, but he would not shame himself by showing fear to his murderers.

"No English?" Longarm asked again.

The man shrugged.

Longarm turned to look around the circle of do-it-your-self justice-bringers. "You should be proud of yourselves," he said coldly. "You're trying to hang some Basques who don't even understand the words for what they are accused of doing."

"Uh-oh," someone muttered from the back of the crowd.

"What was that?"

"I said . . . oh, shit." The man came forward a few paces. "I heard that Norris Smith was buying some sheep outa Idaho or some place like that. He said something about hiring some Bascos to tend them for him."

Longarm sent his stare around the circle of men, but there were very few eyes meeting his this time around.

"We thought . . ."

"Go ahead. Tell me what you thought," Longarm challenged.

"They was hiding down in a draw when we caught them," the man said with a note of complaint in his voice. "They was huddled around this fire, see, cooking a rabbit. A damn jackass rabbit. Now you know as well as us, Marshal, that a man don't eat jackrabbit normally. So we figured—"

"Uh-huh. You figured. And that was your first mistake. Assholes like you get to thinking, you just naturally have to fuck things up, don't you."

Most of them took it. They had earned it. But the man with the rope bridled at the insult. "I don't care who you think you are, mister, you can't talk to us like that."

Longarm raised an eyebrow and took a pull on the crook. He was almost becoming used to the awful things. "You think it would be better for me to let you hang these men?"

"No, but—"

"Then shut up. I'm sick of you and all the rest like you."

The man dropped his rope and looked like he was ready

to make something more of it. He took a step forward. Then he must have seen the ice glinting in Longarm's eyes. He muttered something unintelligible and turned around.

"Untie these men," Longarm said, "and feed them. Where are their things?"

There was considerable shifting and drifting as men tried to get out of the way of the tall deputy's eyes.

"Divvied it all up already, have you? That's about what I expected." He planted his fists on his hips. "Now you can put it back. Right here." He pointed to the ground in front of him.

Quickly the men who had been in the party that originally found the Basques went to their gear and returned to deposit the sheepherders' few possessions on the ground at Longarm's feet. Others untied the prisoners.

The Basques stood where they were, obviously uncertain about what was to happen now, probably worried that they would be shot trying to "escape."

"Is this all of it?"

No one answered.

Longarm motioned the sheepherders toward their things, and three stocky ponies were led up beside the pile.

Cautiously the Basques reassembled their gear and mounted.

The one who seemed to be the leader of the three looked down at Longarm in silence. He had not the words to communicate whatever he might have said. He looked at Longarm for a moment, then nodded. He wheeled his horse into the night with a word to his companions, and the three rode away, breaking into a gallop and leaning low on the necks of their horses as soon as they were clear of the ring of men who surrounded them. Apparently they had believed until that last moment that there still might be a gunshot directed toward their backs.

Longarm could well imagine the relief they must have been feeling when there was no sound of gunfire from behind.

"Where is Walker?" Longarm demanded.

"He's . . . he's set up a headquarters, like. Back in Washington. Marshal Deal's been appointed temporary deputy to handle the field posses."

Longarm looked them over until he spotted the man who had been holding the rope. "You," he said, pointing. "You can guide me the quickest way to Washington. And when this is over, if you want some satisfaction from me, neighbor, I'll be pleased to give you all you crave."

The man was not feeling so belligerent now. "All right," he said. He went to get his horse.

Chapter 19

"This is as far as I need you," Longarm told his guide as they were approaching Washington. It was late but a number of lights were burning. They were coming in at the end of town near Sara Hosmer's house. Her house and shop were dark, the windows blank, black rectangles that showed nothing.

"One thing," Longarm said, bringing his horse to a halt. "You wanted a piece of me earlier this evening. Do you still want to try your luck?"

The man turned his face away. Longarm never had gotten his name and did not particularly care to now. "No," he said.

"Good night, then." Longarm booted the horse forward, leaving the man with the quick rope behind.

The fellow had certainly been eager enough for a hanging to begin with. But finding out who the prisoners were trimmed his sails for him in a big hurry.

Basic human nature, Longarm thought. However wrong or misguided, a man does not *want* to go out and make mistakes—any mistakes—and deadly ones most of all.

The hanging of an innocent man was not the sort of error that could be corrected. Once a mistake like that was known it would haunt the vigilante for every bit as long as it would be remembered by the victim's family.

Longarm was not really surprised that his unwilling guide no longer felt on the prod. Now all the man would be wanting to do would be to go back to his home and try to forget the entire experience. If he was lucky he would find a way to pretend that none of it had ever happened. And in this case the very worst would be that he would have to tell himself that he and his friends had *almost* made a mistake. He and the others would be able to take much comfort from knowing that no real harm had been done on Fat Woman Creek.

Longarm rode into Washington hoping that the other groups of searchers would be able to find similar comfort in the weeks ahead.

He rode past two saloons that were open, then the Union Pacific depot on the one side and across from it the hotel with a low-trimmed night lamp left burning inside the lobby for late arrivals.

The thought of a drink of good Maryland rye, a proper smoke, the comfort of a real bed was enticing. But not tempting. Not yet. Tonight he had other things to tend to first.

He found the town marshal's office in the next block and guessed that Walker would have his headquarters there.

As at the hotel, there was a night lamp burning inside with the wick turned low to a meager flame.

Longarm dismounted and tied Ron Deal's horse at the empty rail in front of the office and crossed the sidewalk. The office door was unlocked, so he let himself inside.

The front office area was empty, but a small table at the side of the room was littered with dirtied coffee cups, and the floor was badly in need of sweeping. Cigar and cigarette butts had been discarded there so often that it would have been difficult to take a step without treading on the trash.

Longarm turned the night light up and called out. There was no answer so he tried it again and was rewarded a moment later by the sound of someone stirring in the back, where he presumed the cells would be.

"Anybody on duty here?" Longarm asked loudly.

"Keep your britches on, damn it."

Sheriff Harlan Walker fumbled his way to the door and opened it to stand blinking in the sudden light.

The sheriff was barefoot and was wearing only his unbuttoned trousers and union suit. He was, in fact, dressed very much the way Timmy Ryan and Sam Dolan had been when Walker and company took them in the night.

The man blinked again and rubbed at sleepy eyes.

Then recognition hit him, and his eyes widened. "You!"

"Good evening," Longarm said mildly.

Walker fumbled at his waist, but he was wearing neither belt nor gun there.

He went pale and looked as though he would have run, except that he was too frightened to move. Cold sweat beaded on his forehead, and the heavyset sheriff began to gasp for breath.

Longarm gave Walker a cold stare and pulled out his wallet.

"Let me introduce myself," he said in a voice that could have frozen the Mississippi from bank to bank and from wavelet to deepest mud.

It took Walker a moment to grasp what Longarm was telling him. Then he stumbled forward, his breath coming in heavy gasps that hinted at poor health, to take a seat behind the desk.

He examined again the credentials Longarm had handed him.

"You should've told us," Walker said finally. His voice held a note of accusation, as if now this whole affair could be laid to Longarm's blame.

"I had my reasons," Longarm said, unwilling to explain to this rural nobody just what those reasons had been. Although in truth, by now Longarm would have had to agree with the man on that point at least. Longarm was not immune from error any more than Walker was.

"But . . ."

Longarm pulled a chair in front of the desk and helped himself to a seat. He took out one of Thompson's rum crooks and lighted it, tossing the spent match into the rest of the litter on the floor.

"Those boys you were fixing to hang," Longarm said. "They were no more part of the robbery gang than I was."

"But I was so *sure* . . . I'd of swore they were with the gang."

"Unfortunately, I believe you. You would have sworn to it."

Something, perhaps a last remnant of hope, flared in Walker's eyes. "How d'you know they *wasn't* part of the gang?" he demanded.

"Isn't it better to ask why you thought they were?" Longarm returned. "You're sworn to uphold the law, Sheriff. That includes the part that says a man has to be figured innocent unless it's proved otherwise."

"But there they were, damn it. Right there. They had no business t' be out there."

"Of course they did. Anybody did." Longarm took another pull on the poor cigar. "If some lady gets molested down at the end of the block, Sheriff, does that make me guilty of doing it just because I walk down the same street ten minutes later? Of course it doesn't. No more than it points a finger at those two boys just because they'd stopped the night in front of your chase. But that's enough of this talk. I know where one of them is, safe, fortunately. How about the other? The one that got shot the other night? I've heard that he lived and I've heard that he didn't. Which is it?"

Longarm knew the answer even before Walker spoke. The sheriff was peering down at his fingernails and not at

Longarm when he answered the question.

"The thing is...well...Bill Harris shot him. You know about that."

"Yes."

"Put a load of birdshot into him. Didn't kill him right off."

So far that tallied with what Charlie Tweed had said.

"He looked t' be getting better. So Ron was gonna bring him back here and put him in the jail t' make sure he couldn't get away. We got a special work train laid on out of Omaha. Loaded him on at Fairo to carry him over here. He got to bleeding or somethin' on the way. I guess the movement was too much for him. He was dead by the time they got here."

Longarm's face hardened. That, by damn, was just the sort of stupid mistake that could never be corrected. Sheriff Harlan Walker—and to some extent Deputy Custis Long also—would have to live the rest of their days with that knowledge. Sam Dolan died as the result of a regrettable but uncorrectable error. Sorry 'bout that, Sam. If there was a next time maybe the same mistake wouldn't be made.

"Anybody else been killed over this?" Longarm asked.

"No. Nobody."

"There damn near were three more mistakes like that this evening." Longarm told him about the Basque sheepherders who had come so near to hanging, and the sheriff began to look pale again.

"This thing has gotten out of hand, Sheriff. It's gone and run away from you."

Walker buried his face in his hands for a moment. "Yeah," he wheezed. "I think maybe it has at that."

"Pull them all in, Sheriff. It's been days, and still this country is chock full of men who're ready to shoot down or hang anybody they don't know. Hell, by now those bank robbers of yours are probably a hundred miles away and snuggled up to a whore someplace, spending the bank's money and laughing because they got clean away from you."

155

"Oh, no," Walker said quickly. "That ain't so, Marshal. They're still in this country. That's the one thing we do know for certain sure."

Longarm raised an eyebrow.

"Day before yesterday? Day before that? I don't remember right offhand now. But some boys on a scout a few miles south o' town found where the bunch had left the horses they rode during that robbery. Folks in town here identified those horses. Remembered 'em from the robbery, they did. They'd been left at a set of pens that Jess Barkus used to use before the rails came through. The robber gang swapped horses there and changed clothes too. So they wouldn't be recognized, of course. I went down there myself to investigate. Brought the left-behind clothes back with me, and the customers that was in the bank that day identified three sets of 'em as having been worn by the robbers that hit the bank. Couldn't ask the same of the mail clerk on the train that day, because there's no telling where he'd be by now. I didn't think there was any point in asking the railroad t' send him back just for that." Walker shrugged. "But the stuff was theirs, sure enough. When I went down there I took along a fella that used to be a wolfer over in Wyoming. He's as good a man on a trail as is in this country, and he followed the fresh set of horses for me. Followed them back toward town and finally lost 'em on the railroad right-of-way. So now, them having horses and clothes that won't be recognized by anybody, I figure they pretty much have t' be still in this country. They aren't laid up with some Cheyenne hoor, I can promise you that."

Now wasn't that interesting, Longarm thought.

He finished his smoke and ground out the butt under the sole of his boot, then stood.

"Call your boys in, Sheriff. I want you to send riders out. Tonight, not tomorrow morning. I want you to roust your boys out of bed and put them out in the field to call in all your searchers and lay off the alarm."

"But what about those robbers? We can't let 'em get away. You don't know what losing that money would mean to this town, Long. It could ruin just damn near every man, every family, for miles around Washington if that bank fails."

"No one is saying you shouldn't catch your robbers. All I want is for you to quit catching innocent travelers and get down to the business of the law."

"I don't see how—"

"I do. And I'm taking a hand in the case now."

"But—"

"It's my jurisdiction too, Sheriff. I hadn't realized that until you said it was a mail clerk that was held up on the train that day. But it was. Which means I don't have to sit by and wait for your invitation to come in. So it's my case too now, and I figure to have your robbers *and* their leader behind bars by this time tomorrow at the latest."

Walker looked at him as if Longarm had suddenly gone crazy right there before his eyes.

"This time tomorrow," Longarm repeated.

"Anybody can brag, but—"

"This time tomorrow."

Longarm turned and left the sheriff to whatever remained of his night's sleep.

Right now what Longarm was interested in was a drink of rye whiskey, a pocketful of decent cheroots, and about eight hours in a soft bed.

There would be time enough tomorrow to take care of the rest of it.

Chapter 20

Longarm removed his hat, holding it in one hand and the bag he was carrying in the other. He was smiling when Sara Hosmer opened the door to his knock. "Good morning."

"Why, Mr. Long." She glanced past him, out into the street.

Longarm laughed. "Everything isn't quite the way you may've heard." He held the burlap poke up for her to see. "I came by to offer you an apology for disappearing like I did and to repay you the kindness of the breakfast you gave me."

She was still searching up and down the street beyond him, as if she was expecting a posse to appear at any moment with guns blazing. Her confusion cleared a little when Longarm reintroduced himself and explained, "I wasn't wanting to get into that before. Kinda embarrassing considering the way I arrived here. Then . . . well, I expect you heard about the confusion afterwards. That was all just a matter of some fellows letting their emotions run away ahead of their thinking."

Sara Hosmer looked relieved.

"I brought bacon and some eggs and some kinda sticky sweet rolls that they had at the hotel. Or we could go over there and I could buy you a breakfast if you'd rather not cook." He laughed. "Come to think of it, by golly, I could turn a hand at it if you'd lend me the use of your stove."

"You're joking."

"Why, no, ma'am, I'll have you know I can fry a mean egg and burn bacon as good as the next man. A bachelor has to learn to fend for himself." He winked at her. "Though we mostly wouldn't like that to be known."

"This I have to see." Grinning, she pointed him toward the kitchen.

A fire had already been lighted and a pot of water put on to boil for tea, but he was early enough to catch her before she fixed breakfast, which was what he had intended.

Longarm added wood to the fire, building it up to a roar, and then went out back to bring more chunks in to refill the woodbox while he waited for the cooking surface to heat.

Sara Hosmer set the table for two and took a seat, watching him busy around her kitchen. For some reason she kept giving him tiny, half-hidden smiles and trying without much success to hide them.

"Something wrong?"

"Nope. You go right ahead. You're doing fine."

"Course I am."

He checked the firebox, added a few final sticks of fat pine, and set a cast-iron skillet onto the front of the range.

"Perfect," he announced.

Mrs. Hosmer giggled.

Longarm sliced bacon into the skillet and got it to sizzling. Then when there was grease enough he broke half a dozen eggs into the pan beside the crisping bacon.

The eggs hissed and quickly changed color, and the frying bacon popped and spat, making him jump once when a drop of hot grease landed on his wrist. He managed to stop himself from cussing, though.

"You sure are finding this funny for some reason."

"Not at all," she assured him with a feigned look of wide-eyed innocence. She was lying through her teeth and knew that he knew it.

He let the eggs and bacon sizzle while he unwrapped the rolls he had brought and arranged them on a plate.

By the time he turned back to the stove there was a wisp of smoke curling up from the side of the skillet.

"Oops." He made a dive for the pan, discovered too late that he had forgotten to locate a spatula or a hot pad, and had to settle for shoving the too-hot skillet toward the cooler back portion of the cooking surface.

"In the cupboard there. No, to the right." She could not hold it in any longer and was laughing openly now.

Longarm found the tools he needed finally and scooped the blackened strips of bacon and dark brown eggs still running in the yolks onto a pair of plates.

"See there? Told you I could burn bacon as good as anybody." He grinned at her.

Sara chuckled. "Mr. Long, you are a man of your word."

"Every time," he declared.

She left the table for a moment to drop some tea leaves into the pot, then joined him. "I won't say anything about your stove being too hot."

"Good."

A few minutes later, with most of the awful meal gone, she observed, "These buns are really quite good." The sides of her mouth—rather a pretty mouth, he thought—were trembling slightly as she tried to keep back the laughter.

"Thank you." He was willing to take full credit for anything that was edible here, which wasn't much.

"I'll be staying in town another couple days," he told

her. "Didn't want to wake you when I got in last night, but if that offer to board is still good, I'd like to take you up on it."

She paused for a moment, looking at him, before she answered. Then it was with a nod. He got the impression that she was considering something more than just the taking on of a temporary boarder when she hesitated. He hoped that she was, anyway. The widow Hosmer was a very pretty woman. Moreover, he liked her.

When the meal was ended, Longarm headed for the sink and began to pump fresh water from the cistern.

"Don't you dare," she chided him. "If you wash dishes the way you cook I'll not have any china left by the time you're through. You go on and let me clean up."

"I was hoping you'd say that. I'll go find a clean shirt and things. My gear is still where it was?"

She nodded, and he went out the back way to the converted barn. He could see that she had been busy in the shop while he was away. There was now some cloth laid out on the work tables, and some of the pieces were beginning to look like fancy dresses even to his inexpert eye.

He washed quickly out of a bucket of cold water, dressed in clean clothes from his bag, and was feeling much better when he went back to the house.

Sara Hosmer was not alone when he returned. He could hear her voice, sharp and not happy, before he reached the back door.

"You have no right to push your way in like this, Ron. I've told you often enough before that I don't want you here, and now I'm telling you for the last time. Get out of my home and stay out."

"You'd better change your tune, Sarie. I could lock you up for obstruction of justice if I wanted. People saw him come in here, and I know you're hiding—"

Longarm stepped inside and leaned against the doorjamb with his arms crossed.

Sara Hosmer was standing by the sink with soapsuds up to her elbows. Town Marshal Ron Deal was standing on the far side of the table from her.

"She isn't hiding anybody, Ron," Longarm said. "Here I am."

Deal gave Mrs. Hosmer one more hostile glance, then turned his attention to Longarm.

"You're a bold son of a bitch, aren't you?"

"There isn't any need for that kind of language in front of the lady," Longarm said. "We can talk without that."

"We won't be talking long then. I'm arresting you, mister. For horse theft, conspiracy to commit murder, conspiracy to commit armed robbery, aiding the escape of a felon . . ." He sounded like he was willing to go on with the list for some time.

Longarm grinned at him. "Haven't talked to Sheriff Walker since you got back to town, have you?"

Deal blinked. "No." He sounded mildly puzzled.

Longarm's grin got wider. "Just as well that you didn't. If you had, you might have turned tail and run for it. This makes it easier."

"I don't under—"

"While you are arresting me on your make-believe charges, Ron, and maybe trying to arrange it that I wouldn't live to stand trial, I figure to be arresting you."

"Me?"

"That's right, Ron. You. On charges of murder. And since you made the suggestion, maybe I oughta add something like conspiracy to commit murder and conspiracy to commit armed robbery, and—what was that other one?—aiding the escape of felons."

Longarm straightened, his hands dropping slightly lower, a little closer to the butt of the Colt that rode at his waist.

"If you want to resist arrest, Ron, I suggest we do that outside. No need to get Mrs. Hosmer's kitchen messy."

"Who the hell do you think you are?"

"Oh, I know who I am. A deputy United States marshal. And you, sir, are my prisoner at the moment."

Deal stiffened.

163

"Outside if you want to try it," Longarm warned. "And I do wish you'd remember to mind your tongue in front of the lady."

Deal nodded and smiled. "Outside it is, then." He turned his back on Longarm and headed toward the front door.

Sara Hosmer gave Longarm a worried look, but he winked at her. "I'll be back for lunch," he said.

He followed Deal into the street.

"I worry about your judgement, Deal," Longarm said conversationally as they walked out into the street. A few people were moving several blocks away in the business district, but there was no one near to interfere.

"Are you really federal?" Deal asked.

"Uh-huh. But you couldn't have known that. It is the sort of mistake anyone could have made. No, it's all the other things that tell me you aren't half as smart as you think you are."

"I don't know what you're talking about."

"Of course you don't. But you tipped yourself easy enough once I quit running and started to do some thinking. I had a few drinks before I went to bed last night, Deal. Did some talking while I was at it. That's when things really began to add up, though I'd had more than enough suspicions already. It just took a little confirmation, and you were done."

"That remains t' be seen, doesn't it?" Deal reached the middle of the public street and turned to face Longarm. The town marshal wore a .44-40 Remington slung low at his hip with its holster secured to his leg by a thong.

Longarm shrugged. He did not believe that Deal would make a try quite yet. Not until he knew what had put Longarm onto him so he could make an attempt now to cover himself. He would have to come up with some explanation about why he gunned down a U.S. marshal, of course. But then, any accomplished liar should be able to manage that.

Longarm smiled at him again, although without warmth. "Curious?"

"Yeah," Deal admitted.

164

"Mostly it was your stupidity."

The town marshal scowled and his fingers twitched. He was on the thin edge of pulling iron, but he kept himself in check with considerable effort. "I don't know what you mean."

"My point exactly," Longarm said with another smile. He pulled out a slim cheroot. The last of Thompson's rum crooks had been given away—with relief—at the saloon the night before, just as quickly as Longarm had been able to buy a supply of his preferred cheroots. He used his left hand, keeping the right casually hooked near his belt buckle, close to the butt of the Colt that was riding its crossdraw rig only inches away.

"What I kept coming back to, Deal, was that poor old Sheriff Walker was charging around like a man possessed, just as well-intentioned as anybody could be but without the field experience to guide him. That gang rode north out of town, so he chased them north without ever a good look at the ground for tracks or any thought about trying to figure where they might really be going. Me, I was just along for the ride. It wasn't my place to interfere, the way I saw it. But you, Ron. You knew what was what. I could tell that from riding beside you. At first I just put it down to local politics that you didn't speak up and get things going in the right direction.

"It surprised me some that you didn't speak up and stop things when Walker and his town boys wanted to stick poor Sam Dolan and Timmy Ryan with a crime they hadn't done. You put a start to the suspicions right there. Walker obviously didn't know any better. You and I did. So I commenced to wonder about you then.

"Then, after I grabbed the boys away from you, all of a sudden there was somebody blocking us every turn we took. I knew Harlan Walker wasn't bright enough to manage that. He'd proved that when he led the first posse out. So it almost had to be you who'd taken charge of things. My talk in the saloon last night confirmed it. You took over as soon as there was somebody to chase. Somebody *innocent* to chase.

165

"So I had to wonder, Ron, why you were so efficient when you were after us but hadn't peeped when we were supposed to be chasing the robber gang. It was an interesting point." Longarm bit off the tip of his cheroot and spat the fleck of tobacco into the street. He dipped two fingers into his vest pocket in search of a match.

"Then I did some talking with the crew of that work train from Omaha. It seems, Ron, that Sam Dolan looked to be doing mighty well when he was loaded into that car, but he was stony cold dead when he was carried off. And you were the only one riding in that car with him." Longarm smiled. "In case you're wondering, I've already wired Omaha to send out a doctor who can examine Sam Dolan's body and see what the boy died of. Want to lay some odds whether it will've been the birdshot or something like, oh, strangulation, say?"

Deal paled, and the hand he was holding poised over the butt of his revolver began to tremble.

Longarm smiled at him and continued to fish around in his vest pocket for an elusive match.

"Most of all, though, Ron, it was hearing about the horses and the change of clothes found down south. That meant the gang *had to come back to Washington for some reason.*

"Otherwise they might've switched to fresh horses, but they sure never would have bothered to change clothes and leave behind the things that might've been recognizable.

"No, it only stood to reason that they were coming back here. And for damn good cause. A man doesn't pull a robbery, particularly and shoot someone in the course of it, and then ride back to the same town, unless he's got awful good cause." Longarm smiled at him again.

"Believe me, I did some thinking about that, trying to work out what the cause might have been. You might be interested to hear the theory I came up with."

"Theory," Deal repeated.

"That's right. Only a theory until I prove it. Which I figure to do as soon as you're behind bars, where you belong."

"Of course, I got something to say about that. I'm still standing here a free man."

"For the moment," Longarm said agreeably.

"Tell me about this theory of yours."

"Like I said, I got to wondering what would make those boys act the way they had. And I'll tell you what I think it was. I think the whole thing was set up by somebody smarter than any of them—I'm giving you the credit for that much, anyway, Ron—and that they were told it would be safer for them to drop the loot off in town and not carry it with them. That way, if the posse blundered into them somehow, they wouldn't have any stolen money with them, and they could claim they were just loose cowboys passing through the country. Nobody could prove different, particularly once they were on different horses and in different clothes." Longarm laughed. "I'll bet you never mentioned to them how that same little idea guaranteed that they wouldn't decide to ride off with your share of the profits."

Deal's lips twisted in a half-hidden smirk. He looked as though he was beginning to enjoy Longarm's recital now. He was proud of himself and perhaps was pleased to have the cleverness of his scheming appreciated.

It was obvious to Longarm that the man believed himself quicker with a gun than this tall, lean deputy from Denver. Deal was beginning to relax, to believe himself in no danger that could not be sidestepped once Longarm was dead and out of his way.

"So what they had to be coming back here for, Ron, was their share of the money. I worked that out, just as a theory of course, and asked where you lived. You aren't married, are you?"

Deal blinked and looked puzzled for a moment.

"But you have a lady friend." Longarm shook his head. "You surprise me, Ron, taking a woman into your confidence like that. You can't always depend on them to keep their mouths shut, especially when somebody handsomer or richer comes along and wants to take up with them. No, those women will turn on you when you least expect it."

"She didn't . . ."

Longarm laughed and chewed on the end of his still unlighted cheroot. "No, matter of fact she hasn't. Yet. But then I haven't questioned her about it yet either. I expect she'll squawk when I do."

Deal glowered darkly at his opponent.

"Where was the money, Ron? In that wash basket? I never thought at the time, of course, but I've had the time to chew on it since. A woman shouldn't have been out hanging clothes on the line quite that early in the day. She wouldn't have had time to finish her washing by then. But there she was, out hanging wet things on the line when we rode past. And would have been when the gang rode past too. All I thought at the time was that we should've stopped to question her about which way they might've turned. But of course there was more to it than that. She was the one holding the poke, wasn't she? And the boys in your gang riding clear with nothing on them to connect them with the robberies. That part of it was pretty clever, I got to admit. I kinda like it. And running onto Dolan and Ryan, that was just a bonus. Gave old Walker and his dumb townies somebody to think about while you laughed up your sleeve and helped them chase each other around in wrong directions." Longarm's face hardened. "What I *haven't* worked out yet, though, is *why*. Why'd you do all this, Ron? You had a good job here. Things going all right for you as far as I can tell. So why'd you snap over to the wrong side?"

Deal shrugged. "A man gets hungry. A man wants more out of life than a damn badge and a gun. I knew the bank would be heavy with cash that day and the train sitting there at the same time. It was a chance to put a stake together and make a better start of things elsewhere. Me and Erna have it worked out. We'll go east under other names, invest the money, and sit back with our feet propped up. We'll be rich." Deal's mouth twisted. "And you'll be dead."

Longarm nodded solemnly and held his right hand away from his Colt, moving it to shoulder level as though willing

168

to make this a fair draw.

Deal began to grin broadly. *He* would not be so foolish as to move his hand farther from his gun. *He* would not . . .

His grin broke suddenly and sweat began to bead his forehead when he heard the loud *cla-clack* of a hammer being cocked.

Longarm had not moved. His right hand remained high and wide at shoulder level.

Yet now the federal deputy was holding a derringer that had appeared in his *left* hand, as if by magic.

The small but deadly effective weapon was pointed unerringly at Marshal Ron Deal's chest.

Pointed quite precisely at the spot where Deal's badge of office was pinned over his heart.

Deal moaned low in his throat and staggered backward a pace. Longarm did not seem to mind.

"Still want to try it, Ron? Or will you prefer to make a deal, Deal? We can talk about where to find the rest of the gang. Or I can leave you here in the street and go looking for them. Your choice."

"I . . . I . . ." The man was having some trouble getting his throat to work properly. He shook his head violently and shuddered, then tried again. "I can—I can tell you where they are. I'll help you. You—you'll tell the court that, won't you?"

"I'll tell them," Longarm said. He did not elaborate. Deal was willing for the moment to play turncoat on his friends. But Longarm suspected that would have nothing to do with the case when Deal was tried for the murder of Sam Dolan.

In fact, Longarm was going to insist on separate trials on the different charges of robbery and murder.

"I'll help you," Deal swore.

"Good. Now drop that iron toy and come along to the jail. Or try me if you feel really lucky today."

Deal took another look into the muzzle of Longarm's derringer and shook his head.

This was not the town marshal's lucky day.

169

Chapter 21

"Can't we go now, damn it? They might be getting away."

Longarm gave Sheriff Harlan Walker a sour look. "Just hold your horses. They've been hiding there all this time; they won't turn rabbit now for no good reason. And I don't want to move until that confession is signed and witnessed. We aren't taking any chances with this one, Sheriff."

Once Walker had gotten over the shock of seeing Ron Deal in handcuffs, the sheriff had been enthusiastic about rounding up yet another posse to arrest the gang members who had been hiding in Deal's basement ever since the day of the robberies.

The red herring Deal had begun with the chase after Longarm and the two cowboys had turned back on Deal's own gang, making them reluctant to venture out after so many search parties were organized in the country.

They were still there, Deal assured them when he ratted on his friends.

"What about the money?" Walker demanded. The sheriff was red-faced and quivering with rage, and Longarm was not sure the sheriff would offer more than token resistance if any townspeople wanted to drop by some evening and lynch their own town marshal.

"We already made the split a long time ago," Deal said. "Each of the boys is carrying his own share."

"And yours?" Longarm asked.

"Erna has it put away," Deal grudgingly admitted. He was willing enough to squeal on the male gang members, but still was reluctant to talk much about Ernestine Bailey's involvement.

Longarm had not paid much attention to the woman during the one glimpse he got of her, but he did not recall being particularly impressed.

Harlan Walker, though, had been amazed to find her a part of the plot.

"Miz Bailey is a widow lady," Walker explained. "She's been just a pillar of this community. Led the fund raising to start a school. Involved in the suffrage and temperance movements. She's just been a rock. One of my strongest supporters in this end o' the county, though o' course she doesn't have a vote."

"A widow, you say," Longarm noted.

"That's right. Her husband took sick an' died just this spring an'. . ." The sheriff's eyes widened. "Say, you don't think him and her had anything t' do with *that?*"

Longarm shrugged. "That's the sort of thing a good prosecutor can try to get at later. Play one of them against the other and see what shakes out of it."

It was, of course, the sort of thing that a good peace officer could take care of. But there didn't seem to be any of those in the neighborhood. The prosecutor would have to handle it if he was up to the job.

"I'd like a drink," Deal complained.

"Keep writing," Longarm told him coldly. The former marshal—actually, still Washington marshal since he had

172

not gotten around to writing out a resignation yet—went back to the task of formalizing his confession.

Longarm was taking no chances with this one. Deal had been a better-than-average local lawman until he chose to turn the wrong corner. Longarm did not want any strings left lying around for a smart defense lawyer to tug on.

"That's it," Deal said finally, laying his pen aside.

Longarm read the confession through. Deal's abilities showed in the document that would be used to hang him. The confession was as clear and concise as a properly written case report, the sort of thing Billy Vail would be pleased with if Longarm ever bothered to turn one in so nicely done. Longarm grunted and tossed the paper back onto the desk in front of Deal.

"Sign it."

The marshal did so, and Longarm and Harlan Walker countersigned as official witnesses.

"Now," Longarm said, "we can go collect the rest of the trash in Washington."

Longarm made sure Deal was secured in his own jail cell and that two armed guards were posted in the same room. Then he went out onto the street to join Walker and another posse of townspeople.

Some of the men in this posse had also ridden with the first, but this time their passions were not so high. The men acted subdued and had grim expressions to go with their guns.

This time Longarm did not intend to make the mistake of letting Walker take charge. He stepped forward and motioned the possemen to gather around him, leaving the county sheriff to stay where he was or join them as he wished.

"All right, boys. What we want to do is to make arrests, not cut people down. If we have any choice about it, that is. I'll post you around the house, and I want you to pay particular attention to the cellar windows and the storm cellar door at the back of the place. If they make a break for it, that's the most likely place for them to come out. I'll put a heavier guard there. Then the sheriff and I will ap-

173

proach the front door. If we can take them peaceably, we will. If there is any shooting, they'll have to start it. We won't."

Longarm glanced toward Walker, who seemed startled by the notion that he should be at the front of things. The sheriff said nothing, though, reminding Longarm that Walker was counting on these posse members and all their friends come the next election date.

"You men with the shotguns, are you all loaded with buck? I don't want any birdshot carried today."

Two men quietly snapped open the breaches of their double guns and had to borrow shells from others to reload with heavy shot charges.

"Everybody ready?" He waited a moment, then added, "Follow me."

They walked the few blocks to Deal's house, the men silent and serious about their business this time, with no liquor in evidence and no boasting going on.

Longarm took charge of positioning the posse members while Harlan Walker stood nearby with sweat beading his upper lip and forehead. Walker was breathing heavily, but Longarm did not think it had anything to do with the short hike they had just make. Walker was just plain scared.

"All set," Longarm told him when he was satisfied with the field of fire assigned to each of the hidden possemen.

"All right." Walker pulled his revolver, checked the loads in the cylinder, and held it ready in his hand.

He followed Longarm up the walk to the front door. Longarm knocked.

"Coming." The voice was distant. It was followed by the sound of approaching footsteps.

The woman who opened the door was a hell of a disappointment as a seductress. She was plump and round-faced, probably in her late thirties or early forties. She might have been raw hell on wheels in the feathers, but if so she did not look the part. On the other hand, Longarm neither knew nor cared what quirks or odd tastes she might share with Ron Deal. She had infatuated the hell out of him somehow, and that was all Longarm needed to know.

"Ma'am," Longarm said gravely without tipping his hat. "We've come to place you and the men downstairs under arrest. If you would be kind enough to surrender, ma'am..."

Longarm had no expectation in the world that Ernestine Bailey would ever serve prison time, much less hang for her participation in the crimes. Any halfway decent lawyer could wiggle her free on gender and harmless appearance alone, and never mind the facts.

Apparently, though, Ernestine Bailey did not know that.

Walker pulled out a set of steel handcuffs and stepped forward to put them on the woman's wrists. The sheriff seemed anxious to be the one to take physical custody of the prisoner. He pushed his way in between Longarm and Mrs. Bailey.

For just a moment Walker was between them, blocking Longarm's view of Ernestine Bailey.

He saw her shoulder jerk and her eyes squinch shut just before there was the curiously subdued report of a gunshot.

She must have had a weapon in her pocket.

Walker grunted and fell to his knees. As he dropped, a small lead slug deep in his belly, his finger involuntarily tightened on the grip of the revolver he held, and Walker's gun discharged into Mrs. Bailey from a distance so close that the muzzle flash set her dress afire.

"Oh, shit," Longarm blurted.

He leaped forward, racing past the sheriff and Mrs. Bailey for the back of the house, where Deal had said the cellar stairs ended. Neither Walker nor Ernestine was going anywhere for the time being, and there were half a dozen armed men in that cellar who would have been alerted by the sounds of the gunshots.

Longarm reached the kitchen at the back of the house in time to see the cellar door fly open, and a man appeared at the head of the stairs with a revolver in his hand.

Longarm shot him in the chest, and the man tumbled backward, falling loudly down the staircase.

"United States marshal," Longarm shouted down the stairs. "You are all under arrest. If you surrender yourselves now you will receive a fair trial and . . ."

He was already too late. From outside the house, the posse members opened up with every weapon they carried.

Down below Longarm could hear glass shatter as the few cellar windows were targeted. Ricocheting bullets whined and zinged off the stone walls of the cellar, and the gang members began to return the posse's fire.

Another man charged the stairs, shooting as he came. Longarm stepped back out of the immediate line of fire and waited until the man showed himself at the top of the stairs.

"Drop it!"

Instead the gunman spun toward Longarm with his revolver leveled. He did not look any older than Timmy Ryan, and he was frantic with terror.

Longarm shot him in the face, and he snapped backward out of sight.

Beneath Longarm's feet he could hear shouts and a rush of booted feet as the remaining four robbers made a break for the storm door.

Longarm heard the heavy wooden doors bang open, and the gang tried to make a rush for it into daylight and freedom.

There was another sharp round of gunfire from the heavily armed posse members Longarm had posted there.

And then there was silence.

Longarm went to the door leading onto the back porch of the house and eased it open, standing well to the side just in case the posse was still nervous.

"Cease fire!" he shouted. "Cease fire! This is Deputy Long. Cease fire."

Only silence answered him. He waited a moment more before he showed himself at the door.

The four gang members were sprawled on the grass behind the house. None of them had gotten more than five yards from the storm doors. They lay in awkward poses, their bodies riddled with bullets and buckshot, blood pooled around them.

Past them several of the possemen were bent over losing their dinners.

"Fire!" someone shouted from the front of the house. "There's a fire."

Longarm ran back to the front door. Ernestine Bailey's dress had caught fire completely, and the flames were already spreading to the structure of the house.

Men ran inside and helped Longarm tear drapes from the windows and use them to beat the flames out.

Walker looked to be in a bad way, although he was still alive. Mrs. Bailey was dead. Uncaring that her matronly figure was charring under the flames that consumed her clothing.

"You, get a doctor," Longarm ordered. "You and you carry the sheriff out onto the grass. But be easy with him. No point in hurting him."

Walker looked mutely up at Longarm and raised an eyebrow.

Longarm smiled at him. "It'll hurt like hell, but you'll make it, Harlan."

The heavyset man was able to relax a bit after that. He even looked pleased.

Longarm wondered about that for a moment. Then he realized. Now Harlan Walker was not the ineffectual fool who had screwed up the chase for the men who had robbed Washington's bank.

Now Walker was and always would be the brave public official who was wounded in the line of duty, who had recovered that stolen money.

Longarm shook his head sadly and turned back inside to finish the job. He still had to find where Mrs. Bailey had hidden the loot. He did not expect that to be much of a chore, though.

It wasn't.

Chapter 22

"Ouch!"

Longarm jerked his arm back with a quick apology. He had been stretching and accidentally bopped Sara in the face.

"You brute. You did that on purpose," she accused. But she was laughing when she said it.

"Did you know that you're awfully pretty when you're angry?"

"That's a stupid line and an old one, and besides, I'm not angry."

"All right," he said with mock seriousness. "How 'bout this one. Did you know that you're pretty when you're sleeping?"

She smiled. "That's better. I can't even argue with it, because I've never seen me sleep. Come here." She pulled him to her, wrapping her arms around him, and kissed him.

Longarm responded with enthusiasm. The kissing led to something more, so that it was a considerable amount of time later before they made it out to the kitchen and she could begin cooking their breakfast while Longarm brought in wood and pumped water from the cistern.

"There's something you are trying to avoid telling me," Sara said over tea later.

"There is?"

"Don't look so offended, dear. Of course there is, and you don't have to look so worried. You need to get back to Denver, right?"

Guiltily he nodded.

"It's all right. Really it is, dear. Everything you needed to do here was done days ago. And I do understand." She smiled at him with affection. "I won't try to hold you here." Then she laughed. "Heavens, I *want* you to go back. The quicker you do, the quicker you can make those contacts for me. You can't possibly imagine how excited I am about getting my business off to a real start. And with your help at that end, why, there's no telling how far I might go."

"All right then."

"And you did promise to come back now and then. I intend to hold you to that, Deputy Marshal Custis Long."

He smiled at her. "It's a promise I damn sure figure to keep."

"Good."

Longarm turned his chair a little so he could stretch his legs out and leaned back, lacing his hands behind his neck.

Sara had no idea how close he could have come to throwing his badge away and coming back here—or someplace, anyplace, else—to turn into a damned vegetable.

People like Ron Deal would have liked that. But Longarm would not have. Not in the long run, no matter how discouraged he might feel at any given moment.

He sighed. Dealing with the assholes of society was not always a pleasant thing. Nastiness just plain went with the territory.

But, damn it, the truth was that he only got to feeling

like that when he concentrated on the creeps he was arresting and forgot about those other, better people that he was protecting.

Protecting. That was what this business of his was *really* all about.

Protecting people like Sara, who had her few dollars of savings tied up in the bank here in Washington. Or Timmy Ryan, who the last he had heard was still recuperating at the Thompson ranch, and just might well stay on permanently. Or those uncomprehending Basque sheepherders, who would have been dead now if mob rule had had its way.

Protecting people like that was what Longarm did. And pretty damn well, if he did think so himself.

Better than Ron Deal or Harlan Walker or a hell of a lot of others, anyway, if not always well enough to meet his own satisfaction.

So he would go right on doing it—and trying to remember the good reasons for him to be doing it—and Billy didn't ever have to be the wiser about how close he had come to losing his top deputy.

Longarm stood, and Sara glanced toward the clock on the wall.

"I'll help you pack," she said. Then, cheerfully, "Unless you have objection, sir, I believe there should be time for one more, uh . . ." She giggled. ". . . for one more before you have to catch that train."

Longarm reached for her and pulled her to him. "The gentleman has no objection, ma'am."

But it was just as well that she was willing to help him pack, because he very nearly missed the train in spite of their early start.

Watch for

LONGARM ON DEADMAN'S TRAIL

one hundred and sixth novel in the bold
LONGARM series from Jove

coming in October!